OKLAHOMA CHRISTMAS BLUES

THE MCINTYRE MEN
BOOK ONE

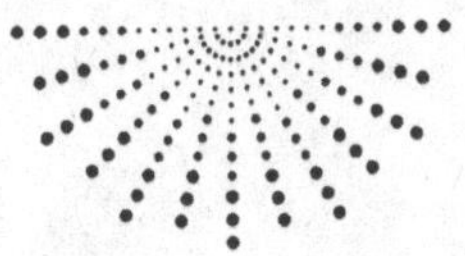

MAGGIE SHAYNE

OLIVERHEBERBOOKS

CHAPTER ONE

$\mathcal{T}$he Long Branch Saloon didn't open for another hour, but how could anyone resist Santa Claus peering through the window, tapping on the glass?

Sophia wiped her hands on a bar towel and went to let him in, and he beamed a smile at her. His dimples were very real, and so, she thought, was his snowy white beard. "Chilly out there today," he said. "I brought my lunch, but I'm craving a hot cocoa to go with it."

"Hot cocoa it is."

"I'll take it to go," he said, looking around. "You're not open yet, are you?"

"Not quite. I'm just getting familiar with the layout. My first day on the job and all."

"Ah, and here I thought I recognized you. You're new in town?"

"Sure am," she said. "I grew up in a small town a lot like this one, though." At seventeen, she'd thought she couldn't shake the dust of her hometown off her boots fast enough. At twenty-nine and counting (loudly, inside her head), she'd come running to Big Falls, Oklahoma like her tail was on fire. Her dream life had crumbled. This small town was the only place where she had family these days. Coming here had been a knee-jerk reaction, an impulse. Whether it had been a good one remained to be seen.

"Sophia McIntyre," she said, extending a hand. Santa pulled off his thin white gloves and clasped her hand in his. It was warm and strong. "You just find a comfortable stool, Santa. You can eat your lunch right here where it's warm. I'll get that cocoa."

She went behind the bar and took down one of the heavy stoneware mugs. "Marshmallows?"

"Absolutely."

Smiling, Sophia mixed and stirred and dropped some marshmallows on top, then set the mug full of chocolate in front of her first customer. Santa pressed his palms to the mug and, closing his eyes, inhaled the steam. "Mmm. Simple pleasures."

She couldn't reply, not having had many of those lately.

"Are you a bartender by trade, Sophie?"

"Sophia," she corrected. "Time will tell, I guess." He frowned at her, but waited for more, and she found herself talking though she didn't know why. "I worked my way through college and med school slinging drinks. It's like riding a bike. You never forget."

"So you're a doctor then? My, my. Small-town girl makes good." She didn't reply, but he went on. "What brings you to Big Falls?"

She shrugged. "I have family here. I don't know, it seemed like the best place to be while waiting to hear whether my license will be pulled for the creative way my ex-fiancé was using my prescription pad."

"Oh dear." He reached across the bar to pat her hand. "I'm sorry to hear that, Sophie."

She glanced up at him, shook her head. "Maybe it's not like

riding a bike. I think you're supposed to be telling me your problems, aren't you, Santa?"

"Oh, I don't have problems. There are no such things, you know."

"No such things as problems?" She lifted her head, met his impossibly blue eyes.

"Absolutely not. Nothing happens *to* you. Everything happens *for* you. That's what I always say. Everything that comes along is designed to help you get where you're supposed to be. If you ask me, you're supposed to be right here. You didn't know it, so life gave you a little nudge."

He sipped his cocoa, his elbow on the bar. She'd seen him from a distance yesterday, when she'd first arrived. She'd been driving her Subaru real slow through downtown Big Falls. He'd been in the park that Main Street encircled, holding court in the pavilion on a red velvet throne. Now that he was up close, her memory tried to tell her he was the same Santa who'd been in her own small town when she'd been a little girl. For just a second, she was eight years old again, sitting on his knee, looking up at him with wonder in her eyes.

But that wasn't very likely, was it? No. Not even possible, really.

"Maybe, Sophie, everything you really want is right here in Big Falls, waiting for you. Maybe you don't belong in New York City after all."

"It's Sophia," she corrected again. *Sophia* was successful, respected and wealthy. *Sophie* was just a country girl with big dreams. And then she said, "You really believe that? A fiancé who's dealing drugs on the side? A criminal investigation and my medical license in jeopardy? All that's happening *for* me?"

He shrugged, sipped, studied her. "What if it was?"

She frowned, starting to think this Santa Claus was, perhaps, suffering from the onset of dementia. Poor thing.

"No, no, hear me out now," he said, just as if he'd heard her thoughts. "Santa knows these things. What if all those recent events happened because your true calling, your true happiness, the life of your dreams, is right here in Big Falls?"

She frowned, tilting her head to one side and looking into his eyes. "I wish that was true."

"Don't wish it." He leaned back a little, sipped his cocoa and put his mug down. There was chocolate decorating the edges of his whiskers. "I think for right now you ought to try *hoping* it. Just hope, even if only for the next few days, that everything in your life is happening exactly the way it's supposed to. You might be surprised." He smiled, and chugged the rest of his cocoa. "Gotta run, Sophie. Children are waiting." Then he slid off his stool and reached into the pocket of his red velvet coat.

Sophia held up her hands. "No. Your money's no good here, Santa."

"Thank you." He smiled at her and something flashed in his eyes, a full blown twinkle so unexpected she took a step backwards in shock. "Believe the way you believed when you were a little girl, and watch the magic happen. Lots of magic around, especially this time of year." Then he winked, turned and walked away.

Sophie—Sophia—stared at the batwing doors long after he'd gone through them. She didn't quite know what to make of the Santa who maybe believed a little too much. And yet she couldn't get what he'd said out of her mind.

What if her life hadn't just disintegrated by chance, or bad luck, or because fate had it in for her? What if there was a *reason*? And how the heck did he know she was from New York?

Small town grapevine. Had to be.

Her three cousins, the hunks she referred to as the McIntyre men, showed up to open the Long Branch for the evening, and she fell into the rhythm of pouring, stirring, blending. She used to be very good at this job, and in no time, it was all coming back to her. She could flip a bottle in the air, spin around, catch it and pour it, all in one move. She started having fun. People were fond of her uncle Bobby Joe, who'd built this saloon, and the family he'd married into, the Brands. He and his wife since last Christmas, Vidalia, came in to watch her work and made a big fuss about how good she was at the job. They'd insisted she stay in their guest room while she was in town. They made her feel welcome. Wanted. They acted like hosting her for the holidays was a gift to them.

A warm feeling started to settle over her. A comfortable feeling. A feeling of...*home*. She hadn't had that feeling since she'd left her own small town all those years ago, after her mom had died. She hadn't even known how much she'd missed that feeling of home, of family.

Maybe that crazy old Santa had a point. Maybe she needed to keep an open mind.

When she got back to the farmhouse, it was late. She hadn't expected to find anyone awake, and went in quietly, so she wouldn't wake anyone up. The place was illuminated by the Christmas lights that twinkled from a huge Douglas fir in the living room and the soft glow of the fireplace. The smell of freshly baked cookies made the air almost taste of chocolate. As she tiptoed through the living room, she spotted Aunt Vidalia in a rocking chair in front of the fire. She was sealing an envelope and she looked up, smiling when she saw her. "Oh, good, you're home," she said. "I saved you a cookie. It's probably still warm." She nodded toward a plate that held a giant cookie. It was on an end table right beside a giant, soft easy chair.

Unable to resist, Sophia sank into that chair. "You're going to spoil me so much I'll never want to leave," she said. The fire crackled and the tree twinkled. She inhaled the mingled scents of evergreen and burning wood, and a hint of peppermint from somewhere.

"That's the plan." Vidalia got up and set her envelope on the mantle.

Sophia couldn't help but notice the name scrawled across the front. *Santa.* She frowned, looking at her aunt again.

Vidalia shrugged. "I write to him every year. Leave the letter on the mantle. On Christmas Eve, put out some cookies and milk. And you know, throughout the coming year, most of the things I put in the letter come to me."

Sophia smiled and said, "Like…a new set of cookie sheets, or a pretty new nightgown?"

"Oh, sweetie, I wouldn't waste my letter to Santa on such trivial things. No, I'm talking about big things. Healthy grand-babies, happy daughters, the love of my life." Smiling wistfully, she crossed the room, picking up her pad of candy cane bordered stationary and her red ink pen on the way, and then she offered them both to Sophia. "You should give it a try."

"What is it with this town and Santa Claus?" she muttered.

Vidalia crooked a dark brow. "You have a problem with Santa Claus?"

Sophia grinned at the intensity in her aunt's eyes. "Not on your life. Gimme that pen and pad."

She took both, said good night to Vidalia, and nibbled on her cookie. And then she sat there, alone in the living room in front of the giant, twinkling Christmas tree, and she did something she hadn't done in twenty years. She wrote a letter to Santa Claus.

Dear Santa,

If it's true what you told me, then that would be…amazing. So amazing that I think I have to give it a try. I'm going to hope that maybe everything that's happening to me is for a reason and that it's sending me toward the life I want. I'm going to hope. What do I have to lose? And I figure I need to get clear on what to hope for. So, Santa Claus, here's the life I want. I want....

There she paused as a million things ran through her mind. What did she want? She wanted her ex-fiancé Skyler in jail. But that was already a given. He'd been convicted of using her prescription pad to obtain OxyContin and then selling it to addicts. He was only free until his sentencing right after the holidays. The problem was he wouldn't leave her alone. She wasn't afraid of him. But he kept calling and when she changed her number, emailing, and when she blocked his email, coming over to her duplex and pounding on her door and not leaving until she called the police. After the third time, she'd stopped sleeping at night.

It was the pounding on the door part that had made her decide to leave New York. She didn't want anything more to do with Skyler. She just wanted peace.

Nodding, Sophia picked up her pen and wrote, *I want such a peaceful, serene life that I sleep like a baby every night.*

That was a good start. What else, what else?

I want my good name cleared, the investigation closed, the police to believe I had nothing to do with any of it. And I want the Medical Review Board to find the same thing. Vindication, that's what I want.

Her only crime, she thought, had been being a little too naive. A little too hopeful. A little too trusting. She'd had everything she'd ever wanted. A seemingly-decent man who wanted to marry her. A respectable position in an elite hospital's oncology department. A crazy salary.

But even with all that, she hadn't been happy. She'd been beating herself up for it, too, berating herself for what seemed illogical. Why not be happy when she had everything she'd ever wanted? What was wrong with her?

Nodding hard, she realized that despite feeling she *should* be happy, she truly hadn't been. And she wanted to be. So she wrote, *I want happiness, true, deep, lasting joy in my life.*

Nodding, she decided this felt really good, this exercise in hope. And she thought maybe she shouldn't have been so hard on herself before. How could she have been happy in the state she'd been in back then? Even before Skyler's arrest and the subsequent revelations. Her job was stressful and depressing. She'd been tied up in knots all the time and hadn't even known it. Not until those knots had started to untie themselves.

The drive back to Oklahoma had been like a full-body massage. Her tight muscles felt looser and looser the closer she got. And when she'd stepped out of the car at Bobby Joe and Vidalia's farmhouse just outside of town, she'd been compelled to heel off her shoes and sink her feet into the grass. She'd taken a deep breath and felt a thousand pounds just ease off her shoulders.

That certainly lent credence to Santa's theory that she belonged here.

Her career was back in New York, true enough. But she did not want to return to the tension she'd been living, unaware. She didn't know what she was supposed to do.

Nodding, she bent over her letter and added, *I want clarity. I want to know what it is I'm supposed to be doing with my life and I want it to be something that I love, using my skills, but without all the stress and tension I had before.*

This was good. Her letter was coming along beautifully. But there was one last thing, the obvious one, and the most difficult. She wanted love. She wanted the kind of love she saw between Bobby Joe and Vidalia. Uncle Bobby Joe was more relaxed and happier than she'd ever seen him. He looked ten years younger. Vidalia, a raven-haired beauty of Mexican descent, who had cheekbones to die for, obviously adored him. She had five grown daughters and would make Sophia number six if she'd let her. She was the living proof that fifty-something was the new thirty-something. Sophia had loved her on sight.

The two of them together were…it just was amazing to watch. They interacted like cogs in a wheel, like they were sharing a brain, and they were a unit that was far more than the sum of its parts. It was supernatural, the power of what was between them. Damn, she wanted that.

To think she'd been about to settle for something that wasn't even close. What a narrow escape!

Nodding, she added it to her letter.

"I want love," she whispered as she wrote the words down. "I want true, deep, crazy, passionate, beautiful, heart-racing, soul-filling, breathtaking love, Santa. And you know what else? I really don't want to go through the holidays without someone special to share them with." And then she wrote a little more. *I'm going to try hoping this really works, just like you said, Santa. And if it doesn't, you're never getting free cocoa from the Long Branch again.*

And then she signed it. *Love, Sophie.*

Frowning, she looked down at what she'd written, surprised to find that she'd written Sophie, and not Sophia. She started to try to make the *e* into an *a*, but something made her stop. She put the pen down. Then picked it up again and added, *PS. Just kidding about the free cocoa.*

Then she folded the letter and tucked it into a plain white envelope. But she didn't leave it on the mantle or seal the envelope. There were a couple of days until Christmas, and she might just need to edit it.

She held her letter to her chest, closed her eyes and said, "Okay, Santa. Here goes nothing. I really, really hope this works. Ball's in your court, big guy. Bring on the magic."

CHAPTER TWO

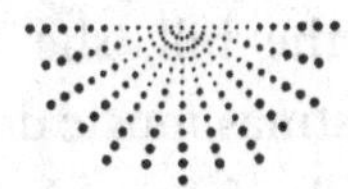

"What we need around here is someone to be the badass," Joey McIntyre said. He was the youngest of her three cousins, and a favorite of his niece and two nephews. Everything was fun to him. Apparently even hiring a new bouncer.

Sophia stood behind the garland-draped bar, polishing glasses and pretending not to eavesdrop on the conversation between her triad of cousin-slash-bosses and the handsome guy they were interviewing for the position. She'd been tending bar for three nights and watching for hints that her dream life was right here waiting for her, but so far nothing. However, she figured seventy-two hours wasn't really long enough to give Santa's method a chance. She'd give it until Christmas. But not one minute longer.

Glancing skyward, she muttered, "You hear that, *Sinterklass*?"

Jason, the oldest of the three, and a natural born leader, said, "We don't need a badass. We need someone who can be pleasant, friendly, and polite, but who can step up should trouble arise."

Right, she thought. A bouncer. They wouldn't call him a

bouncer, of course. The Long Branch was a respectable saloon that catered to tourists, a family-friendly place with an old west theme and dinner theater on weekends and holidays. But where booze flowed, bad behavior often followed. Even here.Robert, aka "the brooder" nodded in agreement with his older brother Jason. "We want someone who doesn't seem all that intimidating—until and unless it's called for."

The applicant filled the bill, she thought, surreptitiously turning the country Christmas music down just a little bit more, but keeping her eyes on the four men at the round table. One man in particular.

He wasn't bodybuilder big. He had more of a whipcord kind of a build, but his biceps looked as hard as iron and that tight T-shirt he was wearing emphasized a chest that some girls would want to write home about.

Not her, of course. She liked intellectual men.

Yeah, cause that's worked out so well for me up until now.

"I can handle that," the man said. His voice was deep, slow and sure. He wore faded jeans, scuffed-up cowboy boots. And that sinfully tight black T-shirt with Johnny Cash on the front, holding up his middle finger.

Classy.

"You might have to learn how to smile, though," Joey put in.

And the applicant, whose name Sophia had yet to accidentally overhear, bared his teeth in something that was definitely more grimace than grin.

"Never mind." Joey turned her way, "Sophia, can we get four celebratory micro-brews over here? I think we've just hired our first bouncer."

"Head of security," Jason corrected. "If our terms meet with your approval." He slid a single sheet of paper across the table.

The man perused it briefly, deep blue eyes narrowing as they sped over the page. He had the blackest hair she'd ever seen. Like a crow's wing. Dark, deep sapphire eyes. He reminded her of a painting that used to hang in her grandmother's house. Elvis on velvet.

Whoa, that was weird. Hashtag, flashback.

The guy looked up at length and caught her staring. Politely, he pretended not to, and slid his eyes away. "Got a pen?" he asked Jason.

Sophia couldn't seem to stop staring until he did. Not her fault, and there was definitely nothing all crushy going on here. He just had eyes like freaking gemstones. Midnight blue sapphires.

Knock. It. Off.

She slapped her towel onto its rack and then reached up high, taking down four man-sized German beer steins with the Long Branch's logo custom embossed on the front. In her head she heard the crazy old man from *Jurassic Park* saying "Spared no expense" every five minutes. Her cousins were freaking *loaded,* and everything about this place showed it. Uncle Bobby Joe had left his Texas mansion behind to live in Vidalia's farmhouse for the first year of their marriage. They'd been playfully bantering about where to spend the second year, though Vidalia was determined not to be "beyond shoutin' distance" of her daughters.

"Sweet tea will do for me," the new guy said, not raising his voice at all. Like he knew she could hear every word. She looked up when he did, and his eyes caught hold of hers again, held on for just a beat longer than they should.

Okay, okay, maybe there *was* something crushy going on here. Wow.

It wasn't because of her letter to Santa, though. It couldn't be. Jeeze, if she started believing in magic every time a good-looking man made eye contact, she'd be in more trouble than she already was, and she was already in a lot.

Her cell phone buzzed. Not a call, but a text. She put one stein back on the shelf and got a tall slender water glass instead.

The sweet tea was in enough demand here that they had it pre-made and ready to serve, so she filled the new bouncer's glass with ice, poured the amber liquid over it, added a straw, and proceeded to draw the three beers from this month's featured microbrewery, Algernon West. Then she carried the beverages all in one hand, water glass secured between the three beers, and a fresh bowl of peanuts and pretzels in the other.

He was looking at her again as she crossed the big hardwood floor—which was so gleaming and polished it had taken her a week to be able to strut across it in heels with any sort of confidence. She was there now, though. In spades. Funny how things came back to you.

She set the drinks down and plunked the snack mix in the middle of the table.

"Darryl, meet our cousin Sophia, best barmaid this side of the Mississippi," Joey said.

"Bar*tender*, boss. Barmaid is sexist," Sophia said.

Darryl got up from his chair, reached out a hand. Sophia wiped her palm on her apron, all the while noticing his long, elegant fingers. They were the hands of an artist, not a bouncer. And when one of them closed around hers, warm and strong, with callused fingertips, while his gemstone eyes locked onto hers, she felt a shiver tiptoe right up her spine.

It had been a long time since she'd touched a man in any way. And he was a fine looking man. That was all it was. Pure red-blooded female reaction there. Nothing else.

"Nice to meet you, Darryl." She tugged her eyes away from his.

"Right back at you, Sophie."

She looked up quickly. "Sophia."

"Got you." He let go, but her hand still felt warm. He nodded at her, and she got the feeling he'd have touched the brim of his hat, if he'd been wearing one. Then he sat back down and said, "When do I start?"

Her phone buzzed again. She headed back to the bar, dipping into her pocket for the phone, then glancing down at its screen. She was glad they were getting some security onboard around here. Oh, she could handle the occasional groping drunk, should it ever happen—it hadn't yet. But in case anything bigger came along, like her ex for example, showing up to make a pest of himself again, she'd be glad of the backup.

The text was from her lawyer, so she tapped it to see the content, her heart in her throat.

The police have cleared you of any wrongdoing. No charges will be filed. I've sent a copy of the report to you at the OK address and a copy to the New York Medical Board. Congratulations!

"Hot damn and hallelujah!" The words burst from her before she even thought to censor herself. She pressed a hand to her chest because her heart was hammering, and her relief was so intense she thought she could float all the way to the ceiling.

Then she felt eyes on her and looked up from her cell phone. All four men were staring at her, but only one with gemstone, sapphire blue eyes and raven hair. Embarrassed, she tucked her phone back into her pocket.

"Good news?" Darryl asked.

He really was handsome. Probably the handsomest man she'd ever seen, and that was saying something, given that he was still surrounded by her cousins, three of the best looking men in the state. The whole country, maybe. She was glad he'd be working here. She couldn't be blamed for enjoying the bonus of getting to look at him every day, could she? Heck, she was looking at him now, wasn't she? Still?

So look away.

I'm trying.

Yes, she talked to herself inside her head. It was not insane. She'd checked with a shrink she'd worked with back in New York.

"Yes, very good news." She didn't elaborate.

"Well, congratulations. Whatever it was." He smiled. Was that a dimple in his cheek? Was that even fair that he could look like that *and* have a dimple? "Bosses?" Darryl said, changing the subject. "I can start anytime."

Sophia noticed then that her three cousins were looking from her to the new guy and back again, their expressions curious. Picking up on her inability to stop staring at him, probably.

"Uh, yeah," Jason said, looking back at Darryl again. "We could use you tonight, if you can swing it. We're always busy this time of year. People traveling for the holidays. My father's a genius, the way he pulls them in. We're a must-see stop for everyone passing this way."

"I can start tonight," Darryl replied.

"Good. We open at five, but you don't need to start until seven. Booze isn't really flowing till then. It levels up around nine. You got a place to stay?"

"Not yet."

Jason got to his feet, which signaled the others to do the same. He was not only the oldest but also the tallest of Uncle Bobby Joe's three sons. He always got to play Marshall Dillon when they did *Gunsmoke* re-enactments. "We've got a vacant room upstairs, if you're interested.

"I'd be glad of it," he said.

"Done. You can pull your truck around back."

"And a sweet truck it is," Joey said. "Damn."

Darryl beamed a little bit. Ah, a cowboy and his truck. That was true love, Sophia thought.

"There's an outdoor stairway," Jason said. "I'll unlock the room and leave the key on the night stand. Just park out back where we do and bring your stuff up whenever you're ready."

The men all shook hands, and Darryl-the-Gorgeous-Bouncer headed for the batwing doors, his long legs eating up the distance in a few strides. He picked up the hat he'd left on a peg near the door, settled it onto his head, tipping the front down at just the right angle, and then he turned back, looked at her, and touched the brim. "Pleasure meeting you, Sophie. See you tonight."

A chill of pure female appreciation tiptoed right up her spine. "Yeah, see you," she said. And then he went outside, and she tried to remember what she'd been doing. Wiping glasses. Right.

"Were there some sparks flying between the two of you, *Sophie?*" Joey asked, sauntering over to the bar with his stein. The effect was ruined by the foam on his upper lip. Because of his fun loving attitude and inability to be embarrassed, Joey played Festus in the dinner theater bits. And he hammed it up, big time.

"I seem to recall punching you in the face for calling me Sophie one summer," she said.

"Well, yeah, but we were younger then. Eight and ten I think."

She shrugged. "Right. I'd hit you a lot harder now."

Joey grinned. "So what was your good news, cuz?"

She smiled so hard it hurt. "The criminal investigation is closed. No charges are gonna be filed against me. Legally, I'm in the clear."

All three cousins whooped at once. "That's fantastic," Rob said. "Now if they'd just hurry up and toss your ex into the pen, we could relax."

"We can already relax, Robby," she said, using her childhood name for him and knowing he'd hate it. "Skyler's harmless."

"Right, except for trying to kick your door in and scaring you so bad you had to call the cops."

"I wasn't scared." She had to lower her eyes, because she knew they all saw right through her. "Okay, I was a little scared. But he's a million miles away."

"Not far enough," Rob said.

He was still sitting at the table, sipping his beer. Of the three of them, he was the hardest to be close to. Closed off and quiet. But then again, he had his reasons.

"So?" Joey asked. "What about you and the new guy?"

"Oh, come on, Joey, the last thing I need is another male complication in my life. And I've got no intention of getting tangled up with a local cowboy while I'm in town. This is a temporary visit, don't forget." Even as she said it, it felt kind of false. So far, she'd been having a pretty good time.

She'd slept last night after writing that silly Dear Santa letter. She'd slept all night long. That was a small miracle.

"You know, cuz, we were all planning to go back to our old lives too, when we first came out here," Joey said. "Stayed on to help run the saloon after Dad almost died last Christmas. And then…then I don't know what happened. Here it is almost Christmas again, and we're still here."

"This place gets hold of you," Jason said softly.

Rob rolled his eyes. "You, maybe. Not me. Soon as I'm sure Dad can handle it, I'm out of here."

Sophia drew a deep breath and released it slowly. Between her cousins and their newfound stepmother, Vidalia, half-sister Selene, and Selene's four sisters, there didn't seem to be anyone in town not trying to convince her to stay. Except for Rob, and that was just because he was too miserable to care what she did.

"I've got a career waiting for me." She took off her apron and hung it on the peg below bar level, out of sight. "I'm out of here until opening time. You guys good with that?"

"You bet."

"Sure thing."

"Do what you want."

Shaking her head, she headed across the saloon, through the kitchen, and out the back door.

The sunshine was a shocker. Inside the saloon with its holiday tunes, glittery garland draped over every surface, and pine scent wafting from everywhere, she'd almost expected to step outside into cold and snow. All the locals were complaining that it was freezing out. Most hadn't experienced a northeastern winter, though.

She would never have thought she'd miss snow. But this time of year, she did. Someone said it had been snowing earlier today over in Tucker Lake, the nearest *big* town.

Maybe it would snow a little bit here, too.

Maybe she'd just add that to her Dear Santa letter. Yeah, right after she crossed vindication off her list.

No criminal charges. Hot damn.

CHAPTER THREE

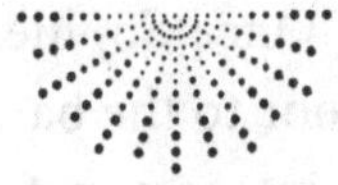

That barmaid was just about the prettiest thing Darryl Champlain had seen, ever. Caramel hair all wavy and wild, eyes as big and blue as a Walt Disney woodland creature. That was pretty much the complete catalogue of his thoughts as he walked out the batwing doors into the cooling weather. Since he'd landed here in Big Falls, Oklahoma, the weather had swung between "best wear a jacket" and "cover all exposed skin." There was a nip in the air tonight, and he pulled on his denim jacket as he walked to his truck. His pride and joy. The payments on it were higher than his rent back in Houston had been. Too bad. He loved it. A cherry 1972 Ford, lifted, supercharged and tuned to perfection. She was fire engine red and he adored her.

He climbed in and sat there a second, the beautiful Sophie still in his mind's eye. Hair tumbling over her shoulders. At least it had been when he'd first walked in. Her smile was huge and bright, but never quite reached her eyes—not until someone had texted something that made her holler. That smile had been real. Damn near blinded him.

She'd arrived a few minutes after he had, coming from

somewhere in the back while he sat there talking to the owners, going over the role they wanted him to play. Jason was the kind of man that other men respected, the kind of man they'd follow. He had that way about him. Joey was laid back, didn't seem to take life too seriously. Darryl knew his type. Out for a good time, footloose and fancy free. Probably hadn't even had his heart broken yet. And then there was Robert. Darryl hadn't figured Rob out just yet. Once Sophie walked in, he'd stopped trying. She crossed the floor to the bar, pulling all those butterscotch and caramel curls into a ponytail on the way, and never looked up. Then she went behind the bar and put on an apron, but not before he'd noticed how perfectly she filled out those jeans of hers.

He wondered if she'd be up for a meaningless holiday fling.

He started the truck and revved the motor a little, because he liked to hear its whine. He'd added the super charger himself and man did it sing.

The "interview" had been a formality staged for Sophie's benefit. Her cousins had hired him before he'd ever arrived at the Long Branch, but not as the new bouncer. His job was actually to watch over her. Apparently, she had a problem ex and the McIntyre boys wanted to make sure she was safe.

It sure wasn't going to be a chore. He'd liked her on sight, and she gave every sign of liking him too. People tended to like him easily. Damned if he knew why. He liked them back, most of the time. This time of year, they could be kind of unbearable with their matchmaking and their we're-not-gonna-let-you-spend-the-holidays-alone mentality. Wherever he went, it was always the same, that notion. He liked being alone. Did his best writing alone.

Okay, he did his best thinking about writing. Truth was, he hadn't written in years now. Not really.

He revved the motor a little more. So he was gonna work closely with that pretty lady. That would almost make all the jingling bells and Christmassy smells, holly-decked halls and glittering balls worthwhile.

Hey, that might've been something there. He took his smart phone from its holster, tapped a button and sang experimentally.

"Jingling bells and Christmassy smells….don't ease the fires of my lonely hell. Holly-decked halls and glittering balls…."

He stopped there, made a face. "Nope. No, glittering balls." And *that* was about the extent of the writing he'd been doing lately. Then he tapped the app to stop recording, dropped the phone onto the seat and turned his truck around to head back onto the road and into town. He needed some fresh shaving gear and a hot meal. As he pulled out of the Long Branch's front parking lot, he saw a guy walking, hoodie pulled up over his head, hands shoved deep into his pockets. Something about him made Darryl uneasy. He'd learned over the years never to ignore his feelings. They had kept him alive in Iraq, barely. Then for ten years as a cop and a handful more years in the secret service before this current hiatus. Traveling the country, taking on private work as he went along. Trying to find something without even knowing what he was looking for.

He trusted his senses. They'd served him well.

He slowed the truck, rolled his window down. "Hey there, pal. Need a ride?" He came to an almost-stop behind the stranger.

The guy just shook his head and kept on walking.

Darryl glanced back toward the Long Branch as he pulled onto the road. The guy in the hoodie was heading toward downtown, away from the saloon.

Maybe he'd come back a bit early. Maybe he'd just grab what he needed at the local store and head back to the saloon for dinner. They served dinner. He'd eat there. The guy in the hoodie had his nerves buzzing a little. And he was here to watch out for Sophie, after all.

He drove back toward town, past a whole lot of brush lots and nothing. He rounded a curve and the road became a small town main street right out of a Norman Rockwell painting. Clean, perfect sidewalks ribboned beneath old fashioned lampposts, each of them decorated with an evergreen wreath. Garland draped from one to the next. Every shop window was decorated, the corners of their glass panes sprayed with fake snow, and their green and white awnings all matched. A big sign hung overhead from one side of the street to the other. It shouted MERRY CHRISTMAS!

And it sounded to Darryl like an order.

An hour later he tucked into his dinner at the bar instead of in the adjoining dining room. This half of the place was deserted, except for her. Sophia. She was tall and elegant for a bartender. Yeah, she wore faded jeans and high heeled boots, a red and green plaid button-down shirt over a figure-hugging tank top. Hair all bundled up. But he'd seen it down. She was a true beauty. Apple cheeks and great big eyes and lips made for kissing.

She seemed at home behind the bar, and yet he didn't think she belonged there. He had to know more about her. The boys had told him precious little.

There were several tables full of people in the dining room. But the barroom half of the Long Branch was deserted, except for her.

Sophie stood on the other side of the bar and said, "Don't you want to eat your dinner at a table?"

"Nope."

"Why not?" She was wiping a spotless patch of the gleaming bar.

"View's better here."

She groaned and made a face. "That was terrible. Seriously, that's the line you're gonna try on me? View's better here?"

He couldn't have held back the smile if he'd wanted to. So he didn't try. "What's a girl like you doing in a place like this?" he tried, making a question of the question.

She shook her head. "Worse yet. How's your steak?" She indicated his plate with her chin.

"Freaking mouthwatering."

"Yeah, the guys have a great cook. Ned cooked in the Navy. Nothing but the best for the Long Branch."

"What made them decide to put a tourist attraction pseudo-saloon in a middle-of-nowhere town like this?"

She shrugged. "Not them, their father, Uncle Bobby Joe. I like to think he triangulated all the ghost towns and other tourist hotspots and put this place dead center. He's a genius at things like that. But the truth of the matter is simpler. He fell in love."

She filled a glass of icy sweet tea for him, brought it back and set it on the bar. "So what's a guy like you doing in a place like this?" she asked.

He smiled. "Funny how that line works just fine on me."

She shrugged. "You're a guy. Any line will work on you. So? What's the answer?"

He thought about it for a moment. "It's just the latest part of the journey."

"To where?"

"Don't know, exactly. It's starting to look like it'll end up right back where it started, though."

She frowned, her brows bending a little. "I have to hear this," she said. "Please, elaborate."

He looked around the place. Still no one bellying up to the bar, and he'd already seen that she didn't wait tables. There were three other girls doing that, maybe still in their teens. She wasn't too busy to talk. And he was enjoying it. "I decided to take a year off and–"

"Wait, wait." She held up a hand. "A year off what?"

He smiled. "Secret service."

She blew air through her teeth like she'd sprung a leak, shaking her head and making her ponytail dance. "Come on, enough with the bar lines."

He pulled a wallet from the back of his jeans and flipped it onto the counter. She stared down at his shield, which was the only thing inside. The wallet wasn't a wallet at all, but a holder for the badge. She blinked twice, then looked up at him. "No kidding?"

"No kidding. I worked for the governor's office in Texas, most recently."

"Why'd you leave?"

He shrugged. "I don't know. I went to work every day, came back every night. After a while of doing the same thing day in and day out, I just got this feeling there had to be…"

She whispered "something more" at the same time he did. He raised his eyebrows and shot her a look. "You know what I mean, then."

"Yeah, I do. This isn't…my usual gig either."

"No? What is?"

She'd been staring off into space a bit, but her eyes snapped back to his then and she said, "We're talking about you. So you decided to take a year off and…?"

"And travel the country. See it all. Write some songs. I decided–"

"Wait, wait, you're a songwriter?"

He smiled. "Not to speak of, no. Was once. Ancient history now. So anyway, I decided–"

"Why'd you quit? Writing songs, I mean? Did you ever record any? Did anyone else?"

He tipped his head to one side. "I thought I already finished the job interview."

She smiled. "I have an inquisitive mind, or so my mamma used to tell me. It's okay if you don't want to answer."

He watched her face. Animated, that's how he would describe it. Her expressions changed with every thought and every emotion.

"I decided," he said, picking up where she'd interrupted him. Twice, "not to use any of my own money. It's kind of a challenge to try to work my way from one place to the next, so I'd have to really experience life in new places, doing new things."

"Wow." She was looking at him as if amazed. "I could never do that."

"No?"

"No. No way. I like to plan everything. I have to know where I'm going and when. I even map out my sightseeing days ahead of time when I travel."

She smiled and he liked it. She had a wide, lush mouth with full, soft looking lips and pretty, white teeth. "How long have you been at this?" she asked.

"Since last Christmas Eve."

And inevitably, that sympathetic look he had come to dread, came over her pretty face. "You left home on Christmas Eve?"

"Yeah, I left home on Christmas Eve. Why does everyone act like my puppy died when I tell them that? It wasn't sad or tragic or heartbreaking. I was bored, and I'd put in my last day and my stuff was all packed. I didn't see why a date on a calendar should make me put off my trip."

"Sure, sure. I didn't mean–" Then she tipped her head to one side and said, "Well, yeah. I did, actually, but I'm sorry. I wasn't thinking."

She tried to act as if she understood when he knew she didn't. But then she asked another question, easing them out of the awkward moment with a kind of grace that told him she must work with people. Lots of different people. "So where did you go first? And where did you start out, if you don't mind me asking?"

"I don't mind you asking," he said, and he thought that was odd, because he would have, had she been anyone else. "Started in Houston and headed west. Up the California coast. Went through the northwest, Washington and Oregon, and kept going clockwise right around the country. East to Maine, then down to the Everglades."

Her eyes were wide, like she was taking in everything about him as he talked. Like she was truly interested. "This is your last stop, isn't it? Your year is almost up."

"That it is," he said, nodding and averting his eyes. "That it is."

"Did you find what you were looking for?"

He sighed. "No," he said softly. "I don't think so."

"Will you tell me what it was?"

He met her eyes again, looked deep into 'em and saw sincerity. She really wanted to know. "Peace," he said. "As best I can put my finger on it, it was peace I went looking for."

"Ah, yeah, peace. That one's on my wish list too. I wrote Santa about it." Before he could decide if she was joking or not, one of the waitresses came over calling, "I need two Margaritavilles and a Bud Light, Sophia."

"Margaritavilles?" Darryl asked.

"One of my specialties. I invented it." She winked and moved down the bar, pulling glasses, pouring from three bottles at a time. He widened his eyes, impressed, and she saw him watching, flipped one of the bottles in the air, caught it, and kept on pouring. She was not just a bartender, he thought. She was not *just* an anything.

"I have to deliver these. The girls are underage."

He nodded and watched her go, thinking maybe a meaningless holiday fling wasn't such a great idea. A guy could get himself in too deep with a girl like Sophie McIntyre.

CHAPTER FOUR

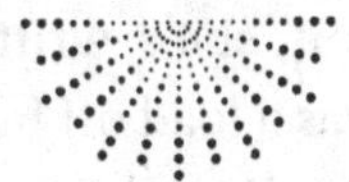

The bouncer didn't have a lot to do to keep him busy, Sophia thought. At least not at first. Things picked up as the bosses said they did most weekend nights. It didn't take her long to get a read on the clientele. Mostly, they were people on vacation, looking for a good time. They tended to drink too much and talk too loud. Then there were always a handful of locals who liked to mix it up a bit instead of spending yet another evening at the local hangout, the OK Corral, owned by Aunt Vidalia herself. They were generally well behaved and decent tippers. Then there were the homegrown players, on the prowl for single ladies on vacation who might want a roll in the hay with an authentic Oklahoma cowboy. The players were easy to spot, because they busted out their biggest, shiniest belt buckles and ten-gallon hats and wore western shirts with way too much embroidery on the shoulders. Their jeans were too new and their boots too shiny. They played up the stereotype. It worked, though. There were a lot of hookups happening around closing time at the Long Branch.

It got crowded from 9 p.m. on. And even then, Sophia didn't think she lost sight of Darryl more than once.

She'd sneaked a peek at his job application to find his last name. Champlain. And in between slinging drinks, she'd Googled him, because she was insatiably curious. Not usually about men, but she was pretty strongly attracted to this one. And while she didn't intend to do anything about it, she couldn't seem to help herself. After all, true love was one of the things in her letter to Santa. She'd already crossed one item off her wish list. And above it, she'd written THANK YOU in all caps. Vindication. That was a load off her mind.

According to the Goog, Darryl Champlain was the one-hit-wonder of country songwriters. He'd written a song she knew. *Christmas Blues* had been recorded by both Garth *and* Reba. He'd won a CMA for it seventeen years ago. There was a photo of some bolo tie-wearing elder statesman accepting it on his behalf. And since then, zip. Nada.

"Hey."

She jumped, shoved her phone into her apron, and looked up with what she hoped wasn't a guilty expression.

Darryl was leaning on the bar smiling at her. "Are we allowed to change up the music? I think I've heard Randy sing Rudolf six times tonight."

"You uh...you got something against holiday music, Darryl?"

He frowned at her a little too closely. She shrugged and said, "It's customers' choice. I can't control what they pick on the jukebox."

He rolled his eyes and slid up onto a barstool.

"Beer?" she asked.

"Sweet tea?" he asked back.

She nodded, turned away and filled a glass. When she slid it across to him, she said, "You don't drink, do you Darryl?"

"Not on the job I don't." He sipped his tea.

She watched his Adam's apple move when he swallowed. "Tomorrow night we've got a band. You'll like that better. We can put in a special request that they do a few non-holiday numbers."

"Thank God."

"So what have you got against Christmas?"

He frowned at her. "You know, you have a habit of asking a lot of questions and not answering any." He was looking at her closely as he said that.

She was saved by an oversized local shouting, "Barkeep! Need a refill over here."

She glanced his way and gave him a nod, noted the empties in front of him, three so far, but he'd been well on the way to happy before his first one. Still, she grabbed another long neck and used the opener mounted underneath the bar on her side to pry off the top as she said, "I'm an open book, Darryl. Ask me anything."

"Where you from?" Darryl asked.

"Be right back." She took the beer to the far end of the bar. Oh, she could've slid it there but Pete Darnell might not have caught it, as tipsy as he was. Besides, she didn't intend to tell the handsome stranger anything, even if he was a hotshot cop-on-hiatus.

She set the bottle in front of the big guy. He was 6'4" and built like a barrel. He had a pug nose, beady eyes, and a blond brush cut rapidly going gray. "You having a good time tonight, Pete?" He was a wanna-be player. For most of the local boys, showing up in their rhinestone cowboy best was an effective way to pick up traveling honeys out for a good time. For Pete, it usually ended in disappointment, according to her cousins.

"Ah, it's dead in here," he said. "And this Christmas music—who can dance to this shit?"

"I haven't seen you dance yet, Pete, no matter what music is playing."

"You haven't been here long enough. How 'bout you come out from behind that bar and dance *with* me."

"Ah, now I'm *sure* you've had too much to drink. Consider this your last call." She turned to go, and he reached out so fast she never saw it coming, grabbed hold of her wrist and pulled her back around to face him.

"Hey!"

He pulled her partway over the bar toward him and then a hand fell firmly onto his shoulder, and Darryl Champlain, his voice a whole octave deeper than she'd heard it so far, said, "Let the lady go, friend."

Pete did so right away, but the look he sent Darryl wasn't friendly. "Why don't you mind your business, *friend?*"

"This *is* my business. And it's time for you to leave."

"I'm not goin' anywhere." Pete slid off his barstool, rising up to his full height. He had several inches and eighty pounds on Darryl. Maybe a hundred.

Sophia didn't want to see Darryl's pretty face get all busted up. "Hey, hey, boys, this is nothing to get all upset about. Pete, you know you've had a few too many tonight. Just sit back down and—"

"You stay outta this, babe. I'll handle this fella."

She blinked. "Did you just call me *babe?*" Then she looked at Darryl. "Did he just call me *babe?*"

"Yes, ma'am, I believe he did." There was a little sparkle of mischief in those dark blue eyes.

"Toss his ass out." She was kind of curious to see whether he could, to be honest. And not too terribly worried. Pete was big, but he was also drunk, and there were three McIntyre men on hand to back their new bouncer up, should he need it. She could see that Jason's eyes were already on the situation from across the room.

"This should be fun," Pete said, clenching his fists and swaying a little.

"Not really." Darryl took hold of Pete's forearm with one hand, turned him around with the other, and then marched him toward the door. The arm was bent behind him and up high enough that it must've hurt a little. Before Pete could react, the batwing doors were swinging closed behind them.

Sophia wanted to run outside to see what happened, but she had customers. She was relieved to see Jason had the same idea and was grabbing a jacket and heading for the exit. Good. Darryl would have backup. Though she had a feeling he wouldn't need it.

When he came back inside, the handsome new bouncer had a baseball bat in his hand.

Sophia blinked in shock when he brought it right up to her and laid it across the bar. "Jeeze, Darryl," she whispered, looking around to see that hardly any patrons were paying a bit of attention. "What did you *do?*" She grabbed the bat and looked it over for signs of Pete's blood or parts of his skull. It seemed clean.

"Uh, not what you're thinking. I escorted Pete to his car and suggested he take a nap in the backseat." He pulled a set of keys from a pocket and dropped them onto the bar. "He was out cold before I closed the door. We'll give him these when he wakes up, if he's sober."

"Oh." She felt a little silly for jumping to conclusions. "So then, what's with the bat?"

He shrugged. "Thought you could use it. Tuck it behind the bar. Try to keep it within reach."

She frowned at him, tipping her head a little sideways.

"What? You're looking at me like you just spotted a unicorn."

Maybe she had, she thought. But no…she'd thought good old Skyler had been a rare find, too. A good, decent man. And then he'd damn near cost her everything. "You're no unicorn," she said.

He blinked at her. "Never claimed to be."

She took the bat, pulled it behind the counter, leaned it nearby.

"You never answered my question. Where you from?"

She thought about lying, decided a little of the truth wouldn't hurt. She wasn't in hiding. She just didn't want to broadcast her whereabouts. "Back east."

"You're being cagey. You're from New York."

She frowned. "How the heck do you know that?"

Three laughing cowgirls crowded up to the bar, ogling Darryl and wiggling their brows at each other.

"Can I get you ladies something?" she asked to get their hungry eyes off him and onto her and then wondered why she cared.

"Rum and diet," the leader of the pack said. "Three."

"Coming right up." Sophia turned and took down three glasses, added a scoop of ice to each, then reached for the house rum and poured it over. The diet cola came last, and she was a pro at keeping the foam down. It was a matter of taking it slow and tipping the glass at just the right angle. While she mixed the drinks, she listened intently to the giggling gaggle over the din of the other patrons. One of them was telling Darryl that they were best friends, and that one was getting married. So the other two had taken her on a pre-wedding road trip, and they intended to have as much fun as they could pack into their week-long party.

Sophia was filling the third glass and tried to rush it, winding up with too much foam. Then she had to wait for it to fizz down before she could add more.

Another bimbo was now inviting Darryl to party with them.

Finally, the foam dissipated. Sophia added more cola, popped in three stir sticks shaped like cacti, and turned to set the glasses on the bar.

"That's a real flattering offer, ladies," Darryl said, "but I'm not much for parties."

"Then what are you doing at a saloon?" Number Three asked.

"Having a conversation with Sophie, here. Or trying to."

The girls huffed, made angry faces, took their drinks and headed back to their table, thoroughly offended.

"*That* was rude," Sophia said.

"*They* were rude. Hitting on me right in front of you like that. For all they knew, we might've been together."

Sophia blinked. "We're not."

"So back to the question."

She shook her head. "We'll just keep getting interrupted."

"Only an hour till closing time. How about we finish up then?"

"Sure. We can chat it up while I close shop. But first, tell me this. How do you know I'm from New York?"

He wiggled his eyebrows and didn't answer.

Huh. Well, crap. She guessed a woman who wanted to keep things to herself ought not be talking to a law enforcement type, should she?

"One hour till closing!" Joey McIntyre shouted over the sudden silence. Everyone looked his way to see him standing by the juke box with the power cord in one hand. "And you know what that means."

Darryl had started to walk away from the bar, but he turned back, looking almost nervous, and asked, "What does that mean?"

She smiled, pointed toward the giant pine tree in the corner, twelve feet tall and barely a needle undecked. The waitresses gathered around the tree. The cook, a live-action version of Popeye named Ned, emerged from the kitchen and made a beeline for the tree, and as he went, he began to sing the opening words of Silent Night in deep and raspy tones.

"Carols," Sophia said. "Last hour before closing, every night during the week before Christmas. You can't beat 'em, Darryl. May as well join 'em." She headed around the bar, took hold of his forearm, and tugged him along beside her to join the crowd around the tree. A few people stayed at their tables, but most joined in.

She joined, singing softly, and glancing up at Darryl.

He was staring at the tree but not really singing. It looked to her as if his thoughts were very far away.

CHAPTER FIVE

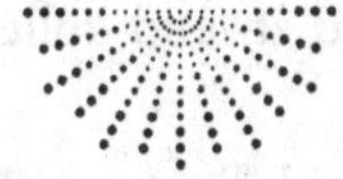

"So?" she asked later, picking up a chair and putting it upside down on top of a round table. "How did you know I was from New York?"

The bar was empty and she'd taken pity on Darryl and left the juke box unplugged after the last customers had gone home. He was manning a big mop and bucket and humming something unfamiliar, but he stopped to answer her question. "I saw the plates on your car."

"How'd you know which car was mine? The lot must've been full last night."

"Saw it earlier when I was here for the interview. Three states were represented in the lot then. And I was pretty damn sure you weren't from Texas or Oklahoma."

"I am actually." He sent her a questioning look. "From Oklahoma. Just haven't been back in a while." Before he could ask why not, she went on. "So why did you ask me where I was from if you already knew?" "Wondered if you'd tell me."

"What made you wonder that?" The chairs were all up and the floor swept. She moved behind the bar, but she'd already washed the glasses, and the guys had emptied the register before going to bed. Jason was renting a place just outside of town, but the other two kept rooms upstairs. There wasn't a lot left to do.

"Because you're hiding something."

She lifted her brows and stared at him. "Is it that obvious?"

"To a guy who's been in law enforcement for fifteen years, yeah. Probably not to the general public though. But I gotta tell you, you've got me curious." He swung the mop around the last dry bit of floor, bucketed it, and rolled the whole thing back toward the kitchen.

"I'm not hiding," she said. "Just avoiding."

"But you don't want anyone to know where you are."

"What makes you think that?"

He shrugged. "Cop sense?"

"Is that a real thing?"

"You tell me," he said.

Then she smiled, because he was pretty good at this game, and looked him dead in the eyes. "I'll tell you what…you tell me why you hate Christmas so much and I'll tell you what made me come down here."

He blinked.

"I mean, you would think a guy who won a CMA for a country Christmas song would be just about the biggest fan Santa could have, wouldn't you?"

He walked right up to her, stood real close and looked her in the eye.

She shrugged and smiled a smug little smile. "See? You're not the only one with cop sense."

"At least not the only one with access to the internet," he said. "But I'm flattered you were checking me out, ma'am."

"I wasn't checking you out!"

"Yeah, you were."

"Yeah, I was." She lowered her head. God, was she blushing?

"How long you in town for, Sophie?"

"A few more weeks. Not long."

"There now, that's something we have in common. I'm not here for long either."

"How long?" she asked.

"A few weeks."

"Isn't that coincidental?" she asked, but her throat was going dry.

"I'd call it more…convenient."

"Convenient?"

He nodded. "Very. I mean, I like you. You're easy on the eyes, smart, funny, and kind of fascinating. And uh…while I'm not looking for anything…complicated, I think I'd enjoy spending a little time with you. While I'm here. And you…."

He didn't finish. Leaving it up to her. She said, "Well, I'm definitely not looking for anything complicated, either. Or anything at all, really."

"But…?"

"But, you may or may not be aware of this, but you're kind of a hottie. And you just about melted me with all those compliments, and I got the feeling they were sincere."

"They were. Are."

"And uh…you know, since we're both only here a short time…yeah, maybe we could…hang out." She shrugged. "Beats being alone for the holidays."

He was quiet for a beat too long, then said, "You know, it just might at that."

"I'd like to know your story, though," she said.

"I'd like to know yours, too. So why don't you let me walk you home, and …we'll see how it goes?"

She smiled wide, and said, "I'm all the way out on the other side of town. It's too far to walk. You?"

"Guys rented me a room upstairs," he said. He sounded disappointed, and she thought he might've been hoping to get lucky and hoped this was more to him than a holiday fling. And yet, not too much more, because she wasn't ready for that.

"How about breakfast?" she asked. "We can meet at the diner downtown. Say eight?"

"Say nine," he said.

"All right. Nine it is."

Sophia locked up and headed out to her car. She was feeling happier than she'd felt in a long time. The excitement of a new… attraction. A new romance, even a temporary, just-for-fun one, had her feeling bubbly and light on her feet—as if the butterflies in her chest were lifting her.

She hopped into her car and started the engine, but before she could shift into gear, pulled out her phone and tapped the voicemail icon, expecting a message from Aunt Vidalia, who liked her to call when she was leaving the saloon, "just in case." The woman had made Sophia feel like one of her own, and the five daughters of Vidalia Brand McIntyre had treated like a long-lost sister.

It felt good to have six adult women who considered her family. It felt really good.

She tapped the play button on the phone and left it lying on the passenger seat.

"Hello, Sophia, it's Dave Ruddman."

Her lawyer again. She hit the brakes and stared at the phone, holding her breath.

"Thought you'd want to know the medical board's findings came in. You've been cleared. Your license is safe. Your record remains clean."

"It's over," she whispered. Then she closed her hands around the steering wheel and lowered her head onto it. "It's really over."

So much relief flooded her that she was limp for a minute or two. But finally, she took a deep breath, lifted her head, and put the car into gear. "That's two things off the list, Santa," she said and then her eyes went wider. "Three! I'm sleeping at night again." She blinked and said, "Four! I didn't want to be alone for the holidays and now I won't. Wow. You know, you've almost got me believing, Mr. Claus."

She turned on the radio, tuned it to XM Holly. Mariah Carey came on, and she smiled. What if everything really *was* happening just the way it was supposed to? She'd been engaged to a man she didn't love, didn't even know, as it turned out. And now she wasn't. She'd been restless and unfulfilled by her life. Now she was standing at the threshold of a new life. She'd been unhappy and stressed out in her work, and now she was relaxed and enjoying herself. She'd been so tense for so long she'd started believing it was her normal state. But now she was uncoiling, every day a little more, as Big Falls seeped into her like warm honey. Soothing and sweet.

She drove around the big bend and into the tiny "downtown" area. It was maybe a quarter mile stretch of road with shops and businesses along both sides. Most of the storefronts bore green and white striped awnings, and all of them were decked out for the holidays. She couldn't drive through this area without a little rush of that Christmassy feeling welling up inside. That swelling in the chest that radiates outward like sunbeams. That feeling had been a stranger to her for so long she'd almost forgotten it. But now that it had returned, it was as familiar as...as coming home.

Big Falls was the perfect place for her, she decided. She was sleeping at night again. What more evidence did she need?

But what about her career? She didn't want to serve drinks for the rest of her life. She was a doctor. She wouldn't feel fulfilled if she wasn't using her gift.

The road split in the middle, circling around the park and meeting again on the other side. The park was a big round, grassy place with a giant pine tree all decked in lights right in the center. The lights twinkled, illuminating a rust and red pickup truck that looked like a relic from the 50's. It bore a bumper sticker that lit up when Sophia's headlights hit it. It said, "Just breathe. I've got this." Beside the text was an image of a hand making the 'ok' sign against a cloudy blue sky.

Slowly, Sophia exhaled. All the breath in her lungs just eased out of her, and the last bit of tension seemed to leave her along with it.

She was sitting still in the middle of the road, gazing at the glittering tree and green park. Experimentally, she breathed in, slow and deep. And then she breathed a little deeper. Her muscles unclenched. She smiled.

A few lazy snowflakes drifted down. She followed one with her eyes as it swooped to and fro, looped up and down again, and then landed on the old truck's windshield. Santa was at the wheel, grinning at her.

She jumped so hard she bumped her head. Then he waved at her. She waved back and pressed on the gas.

Either there was something magical but very real going on here, or she was losing it.

As she circled around the park to the other side, she noticed someone sitting on the park bench in a shadowy spot where the Christmas tree lights didn't reach. His shoulders were hunched, his head down, and his face completely hidden within the dark blue hood of the sweatshirt he wore. He wasn't moving, and she wondered briefly whether he was planning to sleep there.

But that was crazy. Big Falls didn't have homeless people.

Twenty minutes after Sophie had driven away, a pickup truck pulled into the parking lot, its headlights moving slow across the empty barroom. Darryl was still downstairs. He'd decided on an ice cold, long-necked nightcap, because he knew he wasn't going to sleep. The notion of "hanging out" with Sophie McIntyre had him stirred up in a way he hadn't been in a long time. And when she'd said what she had, about it being better than being alone for the holidays, he'd had a moment of revelation.

As much as he'd always denied it, as much as he'd always hated to hear his friends pointing it out to him with pity in their voices, it did stink being alone during the holidays. It really did.

This was going to be the most pleasant Christmas he'd spent in a long, long time. Maybe he'd try to stop being a humbug and embrace it.

As he was thinking all that, the person who'd pulled in started tapping on the front door.

Surprised, Darryl got up, taking his beer with him. He'd assumed it was one of the McIntyres coming by to make sure the place was all buttoned up for the night. But they'd have had a key.

He went to the door, and looked out just to be safe. A smiling face sporting a full, snow-white beard looked back at him. He had eyes that crinkled at the corners, and plump rosy cheeks. He wore lined flannel jacket, red plaid. Just looking at him made Darryl smile, and then when he noticed a couple of snowflakes landing on the old man's shoulders, he smiled even more, and opened up the door. "We're closed, but if I can help you with something...."

"I'm making a habit of showing up here outside of business hours," he said, and he chuckled softly. "I actually have something for Sophie. Do you suppose you could give it to her for me?"

"Sure. I'll see her first thing in the morning."

"Wonderful, wonderful. Just tell her it's to thank her for the cocoa. She'll understand." He tugged a plain white envelope, business sized, from his pocket and handed it over. "Thank you very much, young man."

"It's Darryl."

"I know. Merry Christmas," he said. "If you're lucky, she'll share." He gave a wink, then he turned and headed back to his rusty old pickup truck, got in, and drove away.

Darryl closed the door and eyed the envelope, curious as hell.

CHAPTER SIX

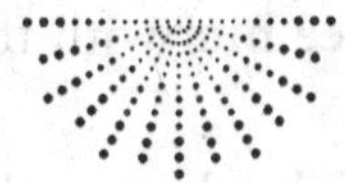

$\mathcal{T}$he stranger was still on the park bench the next morning when Sophia, after her best night's sleep yet, arrived at the Big Falls Diner for her breakfast date with Darryl. She watched the poor soul for a moment. He wasn't moving, but he wasn't in the same position he'd been in last night, so she was pretty sure he was alive. Probably just sleeping.

Resolutely, she headed into the Diner.

"Morning, Sophia," called the cheerful redhead behind the counter. "Pick any table you want, like always. I'll bring the coffee over."

"Morning, Rosie," Sophia replied, then she said, "Can I get a cup to go and one of those big gooey looking danishes?"

"Oh, you're not staying?" Rosie opened the glass case, popped the biggest, gooiest danish into a paper-lined bag and laid it on the counter. Then she filled a styrofoam cup, added cream and sugar, and snapped a lid on it.

"Yeah, I'm staying. This is for someone else. I'll be right back."

Rosie looked puzzled, but Sophia quickly took the bag and the cup back outside, crossed the street and went to the bench.

She set the bag and the mug on the bench near the homeless guy, but not near enough so he'd knock the coffee over when he woke, and then she retreated back into the diner.

When she went through the door, the bell jingled again and Rosie stood there smiling at her with the coffee pot in one hand and a fresh mug in the other. "Who is that fella out there?"

"Don't you know?" Sophia asked.

"No. I mean, I can't see him with that hood on, but—it is a him, isn't it?"

"I think so. And I think he slept on that bench."

"Shoot, we can't have that. Oh, look, look!"

She was pointing and Sophia turned to see the guy on the bench sitting up, then looking from the gift she'd left, to the area around him. Not spotting anyone, he took the breakfast and hurried away, heading down the sidewalk and out of sight.

"Well, at least he took the danish and coffee," Sophia said, turning to head to her usual table. She stopped in front of her booth and let her eyes travel the length of the lanky cowboy who was sitting in it already. He rose, nodded toward the spot opposite him. "Mornin', Sophie."

"Morning, Darryl." She slid into the booth. "I didn't realize you were already here. You should've said something."

"I didn't want to interrupt your good-deed-doing."

So he'd seen all that. He didn't sound exactly complimentary about it. Then Rosie arrived and asked, "What'll it be?"

"I'd love an egg-white omelet with every veggie you can fit in, and a little bit of cheddar cheese," she said.

"Perfect. And how about you, handsome?"

He smiled at the compliment. "I'll have what she's having," he said. "Only instead of egg whites, I want the yolks included, and instead of every veggie, make it ham, bacon and sausage, and instead if a little bit of cheddar, I'd like a lot. And some mozzarella."

Rosie was laughing softly. "You want toast?"

"Yep. Heavy on the butter. Oh, and some home fries on the side."

"One heart-attack special, coming right up," Rosie said with a grin as she walked away. She never bothered writing orders down, just remembered them.

"You keep eating like that, you'll die young," Sophia said, sipping her coffee and leaning back in the soft, padded seat.

"You're one to talk. Your habits aren't exactly healthy."

She frowned, confused. "What are you talking about? A veggie egg white omelet is–"

"That's not the unhealthy habit I was referring to." He glanced toward the door.

"You mean buying breakfast for that homeless guy?"

"Big Falls doesn't have homeless guys," he said. "At least, that's what I've heard."

"I thought the same thing," she admitted. "But he was sleeping on that bench, and–"

"And you should be more careful. Especially with your situ…." He stopped there. Shrugged.

Sophia tipped her head to one side. "Especially with my situation?" She narrowed her eyes on him. "What is it you think you know about me, Darryl? Did my cousins say something to you?"

He lifted his brows, the picture of innocence. "About what?"

"About me. Come on, cough it up, what do you know?"

He held up both hands, leaning back as far as the seat would allow. "I'm not sure what you're accusing me of, but I guarantee you, my opinion that women ought to be careful of strangers comes from nothing more than a healthy level of common sense and a lot of years in law enforcement."

She squinted at him and he looked away. For the first time, she got an odd feeling up her spine. She was not afraid of her ex. But she wouldn't put it past him to send someone to track her down and report back to him. What did she really know about Darryl Champlain, after all?

"So what brought you to Big Falls, anyway?" she asked.

"Are we back to that again? I thought maybe I could be the one asking questions today."

"Mm. Yeah, no. I don't think so."

He frowned at her. "Your happy-holiday mood seems to have shifted, Sophie."

"Sophia," she corrected.

"I hope it wasn't something I said."

She focused on sipping her coffee and wondered if she was just being paranoid. But who was she kidding? She'd never been paranoid a day in her life.

He was right about one thing. Women ought to be a careful of strangers.

"I have something for you."

"You do?" She was surprised. He took out an ordinary white envelope and laid it on the table between them. "What is it?" she asked, reaching to pick it up.

"I don't know. It's not from me. It's from uh…well, he didn't leave a name, but he looked like an off-duty Saint Nick. He said it was to thank you for the cocoa."

Her smile was instant and full blown. "It's from Santa? Where did you see him?"

"He showed up at the Long Branch after hours to leave it for you."

She frowned. "How odd. I saw him at the park as I was driving home last night. I'm sure he saw me too. He waved. He could've given it to me himself, whatever it is."

"Yeah, he could. Another stranger to be wary of, Sophie."

"I am not afraid of Santa Claus," she said. "That man *knows* things." She tore the envelope open, eager to see what was inside.

"He said if I was lucky, you'd want to share. I gotta admit, I'm dying of curiosity here," Darryl said.

She pulled out the contents, two rectangles, obviously tickets of some kind. Her eyes sped over the green and red, holly and berry background to read the words typed across the front, and then she looked past the tickets at Darryl's eager eyes. "Tickets to the Haggerty House Holiday Hootenanny."

"The what now?" he asked.

Feeling a little bit nervous, she read the small print out loud. "'A Christmas ball, country style. Put on your best duds and join us for a prime rib dinner, drinks, dancing, and door prizes. Seven to midnight.'"

Rosie brought their breakfasts, saw the tickets, and beamed. "Oh, you're going to the Haggerty House Holiday Ball?"

"Holiday Hootenanny, you mean," Darry corrected her with a wink that made her beam brighter.

"I haven't decided yet," Sophia said. "Have you ever been, Rosie?"

"No, darlin', but it is the event of the season. Everyone who's ever been has raved. You have to go. How did you get tickets? It's usually sold out before Halloween."

"Friends in high places." North Pole high, she thought.

Rosie left again, and they sat there with their breakfasts in front of them, delicious smells wafting up and making her mouth water. She looked at Darryl, meeting his eyes for the first time since she'd opened that envelope. "It's tonight," she said softly.

"We um…both have to work tonight."

"Well, I do have *some* pull with our employers." She was trying to read his level of interest. Was he hoping she'd ask, or dreading it? "Is this the kind of thing you'd maybe…enjoy?"

"Are you asking me to the ball, Cinderella?"

"I guess I am."

He smiled, a slow, sexy smile that sent a chill right up her spine. "As a rule, I avoid all things Christmassy. But we did agree to spend the holidays together, didn't we?"

"We did. I've thought about a thousand times that the only

good thing about my former relationship with Skyler was that I had someone to do Christmas with."

He nodded. "I know that feeling. Being single at holiday time seems to make everyone you know throw a pity party."

"And try to fix you up while you attend," she said.

He nodded hard. "With people who are so far off the mark—"

"You start to wonder if your friends know you at all—"

"Or if they just latched onto the first single person they ran into," he said. Then he grinned. "At least we got to pick our own holiday pity dates."

She laughed softly. "We did, didn't we?"

He reached across the table and took her hand. "I would be honored to escort you to the Haggerty House Holiday Hoedown."

"Hootenanny," she corrected.

"Gesundheit," he replied.

They both laughed. She said, "I don't think I brought anything suitable for a ball."

"Me either. I guess we'd better shop."

"I know right where to shop, too," she said. "The closet of one Edain Brand Armstrong, former super model and now my very own cousin-in-law."

"I believe I will err on the side of the menswear shop in town. They've gotta have something."

"I don't know. It's short notice."

"Have a little faith. I could make a feedbag look good." He sent her a playful wink, and then tucked into his breakfast.

Sophie started in on hers too, and it was delicious, and cooling too fast. Then again, she'd kind of forgotten about her food, so lost in conversation with him. And then, in between bites of omelette and sips of coffee, he paused to say, "What do you know about this jolly old bearded man, by the way?"

She finished chewing, took a drink of water. "He plays Santa in the park. Vidalia says he's been doing it for years. Why do you ask?"

He shrugged. "Just my nature. Stranger, befriends the new girl in town, gives her tickets to a big event. Sets my antennae to quivering a little."

She set her fork down carefully, took a deep breath, met his eyes. "Look, Darryl, I know we both said we're not interested in anything complicated, so this probably goes without saying, but...don't get all protective, okay?"

He blinked, for the first time apparently speechless. "I don't...I mean...why not?"

"Because it feels kind of controlling. A little bit demeaning, too."

He leaned back in his seat. "You're gonna have to explain that one."

"Well, it kind of suggests you don't think I'm capable of taking care of myself. That the big, strong man has to watch out for the naive little woman, so she doesn't bungle her way into an early grave." It had also been one of the early warning signs that Skyler was not what she'd thought he was—little subtle efforts to control her under the guise of caring. But she wasn't going to bring that up.

He listened, to his credit, nodding slowly. "I guess I can see how it might appear that way from your perspective."

"But...?" she asked, correctly interpreting the open ended nature of his statement.

"But, I hope you'll cut me a little slack. I was a soldier, and then a cop, and then a secret service agent. Protecting people—not naive people or smaller-sized people or female people, just people—is what I do. It's what I've always done."

She tipped her head to one side, considering his words, weighing them. "That's a really good point, actually."

"I thought so myself."

She nodded. "Okay, I'll cut you some slack."

"And I'll try not to act like your personal bodyguard," he added.

"Deal," she said. And then she smiled. "That was great, wasn't it? Just talking it out like that? Being honest with each other and listening to the other person's point of view?"

"It was."

"I never had that before. With a guy I was...you know, seeing. Skyler was always hiding himself from me." She met his eyes. "He was an addict. I think he was an addict before we even met, and I hate myself for not seeing it. Sometimes I wonder if that was the only reason he ever asked me out. I was a doctor. He needed access to opiates."

"If that was the only reason he ever asked you out," he said, clasping both her hands across the table, "then he was a blind, ignorant, stupid man."

She lowered her head, as warm pleasure spread across her cheeks. "I'm not gonna argue with you on that."

He smiled, and their eyes met and held. It was a moment of shared understanding. The more time she spent with this man, the better she liked him. And then he said, "You're a doctor?" as if that part of her sentence had only just penetrated his brain. "Then what the hell are you doing, slinging drinks at the Long Branch?"

She thought about the ugly tale, and didn't want to pollute this pleasant morning with it. "Let's save that for another conversation, okay?"

"Sure. Okay."

Their plates were empty, their mugs drained. "I hate to break this up, but I have an order to pick up for the saloon, and a dress to borrow. Plus, I need to have that talk with my cousins about giving us the night off."

"I'll talk to them with you."

"I've got this," she said. "It's not a problem." He started to object and she held up a finger. "I've got this."

"Okay. You've got this." He smiled, and she gathered up her things and headed for the door.

She felt his eyes on her all the way. And maybe she even added a little swing to her hips that wouldn't have been there otherwise. Maybe.

CHAPTER SEVEN

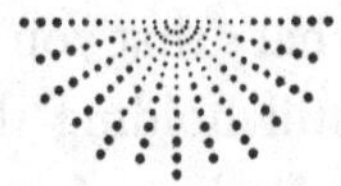

*H*e brought his oversized pickup truck to a stop in front of the big, century old farmhouse where Sophie was staying, the home of Bobby Joe McIntyre and his bride, Vidalia Brand. Bobby Joe was Jason, Rob and Joey McIntyre's old man, and Vidalia was his second wife. There was a story there, but he hadn't heard it yet. Still, the way people caught their breath or touched a hand to their heart whenever their names came up suggested it must be a doozy.

Then he got out and went to the door. He'd picked himself up a dark brown suit with a bolo tie, and he'd polished up his best boots. He had a small box in his hand, and he felt a little bit like a high school kid on prom night.

And then she opened the front door, and he felt it even more.

Her dress was red, and hugged her figure. A plunging neckline held his eyes hostage, because cleavage. And when he forced himself to look elsewhere he wound up with his gaze glued to the slit that ran up one side of the gown exposing her leg to about mid-thigh. She wore a little short silver jacket with it. What did they call that, a shrug?

She said, "Nice suit."

"Uh-huh." He swallowed hard, almost choked, realized words were required here. "I mean, thanks."

She hooked a finger under his chin and lifted his head until he looked her in the eye. He broke free of the spell the sexy dress had cast on him. "Sorry. You look...so good I temporarily lost the power of speech."

She laughed softly. "What's that you have there?"

He realized he was still holding the box. "Oh, right. Um, here." He handed it to her. "In lieu of a corsage."

"You didn't have to..." She opened the box eagerly, though, and then looked inside.

He'd seen it in the window at the little jewelry store in town. A silver chain with a Santa Claus pendant. His red suit was made of garnets, its white trim, quartz crystal. She smiled as if it was rubies and diamonds instead. "This is perfect! I would have bought this myself if I'd seen it." She removed it from the box and handed it to him, then turned around and held up her hair.

He put the chain around her neck from behind, fastened the clasp. She turned again, fingering the pendant. "Thank you, Darryl. That was so thoughtful."

"I knew you had a thing for the guy, so...." Then he nodded toward the truck. "If you're ready, your carriage awaits."

She walked beside him to the pickup and he opened the passenger door for her. "I might need a leg up," she said, "in these shoes."

He looked down again. Big mistake. The shoes were silver like the jacket-wrap-shrug thingie, open toed despite the cold, and had heels so high they made a man want to climb them.

"Darryl?"

"I'm here. Just...calculating how best to...negotiate the truck in those shoes." He was still looking at them, and then tracing the slit up her leg to her thigh. Then he gave himself a shake. "I think I might have made a mistake tonight, Sophie." He met her eyes again. "You are pretty clearly out of my league."

She lowered her head, blushing pinker. "Stop it."

"No, I'm not kidding. You're…never mind. I'll shut up before I talk you out of it." Then he moved behind her, and put his hands on her waist. "Go ahead, hop up. I'll help."

She did, and he boosted her a little until she was settling into the seat. He told himself he should've rented a car.

Haggerty House was a sprawling and elegant Victorian, every roof and window bordered in white lights. A single white candle bulb shone from every window. Gigantic wreaths hung from every door.

The scents of pine and gingerbread greeted them as soon as they entered, and the soft strains of holiday music drew them further inside. A beautiful octogenarian greeted them at the door, "Welcome to Haggerty House," she said. "Choose any unoccupied table you like and let me know if you need anything at all. I'm Betty Haggerty. Merry Christmas."

"Merry Christmas," Sophia replied, loving the place the moment they entered. A spinning mirrored globe spilled red and green lights from the ceiling, painting the entire room and everyone in it, in color. Soft holiday music was played by a string quartet, and couples were dancing on the wide and spacious floor. "Look at that woodwork! I wonder if it's original?"

"Heck with the woodwork, look at that spread," Darryl replied, his eyes were appreciating the food. There were three carving stations, and a massive and lush buffet with everything else imaginable.

"Oh, oh, oh, there's the dessert!" Sophia pointed out several round tables with pyramids of desserts so huge she was surprised their pedestals didn't buckle.

"Do you want to dance?" he asked. And then before she could answer, he went on. "Or can we eat first?"

"So much for a romantic holiday ball," she said, but she was almost as eager for the food as he was. "Let's grab a table before all the good ones are gone."

"Good ones, meaning close to the buffet?"

"Good ones, meaning close to the dessert." She grabbed his hand. "I've got it all picked out." As she wove her way through the other patrons, all of them dressed in various degrees of country elegant, she noticed gowns and jewelry and shoes and boots and hairstyles with equal measures of admiration.

They got to the table she'd chosen, and she let go of his hand, picked up the folded cloth napkin, and draped it across one of the chairs, international signal for "Taken." He did the same, then took hold of her hand again, and tugged her toward the food.

Halfway there, however, he stopped, turned, snapped an arm around her waist, and gave her a spin right onto the dance floor.

She was laughing, surprised, happy.

Come to think of it, she was kind of hitting a new level of happy tonight.

"You tricked me. I thought you wanted to eat first."

"You called my romancing into question, woman. My stomach can wait."

"Ego's bigger, huh?"

"Not only that, but who can resist 'Santa Baby'?"

She had barely noticed what song was playing, a jazzy rendition coming from unseen speakers. There was a corner section of the room set up for a band, and she presumed they'd start later. That was all she had time to notice, because her face was near his neck, and he smelled like heaven.

"I like that cologne you're wearing."

"It's called *Irresistible*. I had to put a claim like that to the test." He looked down at her and wiggled his eyebrows. "How's it working so far?"

"Pretty darn well." He was a good dancer. She liked that she could follow his lead with barely any effort, and the way he threw in a dip here, a spin there, to keep it interesting.

"So you're a doctor," he said.

She had known they'd get back to that. The music changed to a slow, romantic number, and she laid her head on his chest and shoulder, clasped her hands behind his neck, and whispered, "Not yet."

"Anything you say." He tightened his arms around her, and there were no more fancy moves. Just a slow, delicious shuffling of their feet, their bodies melded. His arms around her felt so good. She hadn't felt this way in very long time. Held, maybe cared for, at least in the moment. Desired.

Yeah. It had been too long.

When the song ended, she lifted her head and looked into his eyes and wondered what he was seeing in hers. "Let's get some food now, before you faint or something."

"I'm close, I gotta tell you. It might already be too late." He took her elbow, and they moved to the buffet, helped themselves to warm plates, and moved along, choosing from among dozens of offerings--three kinds of potatoes, six different vegetable dishes, meat and meatless stuffing, mounds of fruit, and big fluffy homemade rolls. They stopped by the carving station with barely room on their plates for the juice-oozing slices of prime rib, then went back to their table to sit down and dig in.

A waitress came by, pretty and blonde. "I'm taking drink orders, and highly recommending Grandma Betty's spiced rum punch. Packs just the right amount of kick, and if you have it early in the evening, it'll be all worn off by the end."

"Sounds good to me," Sophie said.

"What the heck, I'll try it too."

She hurried away, and a second later a tray toting fellow came by to leave their drinks. Sophie took a bite of the prime rib, and it melted in her mouth, eliciting a rapturous "mmmm" that was unpreventable.

Darryl smiled. "You keep changing the subject when I ask about your work. Should I stop asking?"

She finished chewing, sipped the drink, widened her eyes. Then said, "No. Actually, I should get it over with. My fiancé the addict was using my prescription pad to obtain opiates, both for his own use, and to sell. And he got caught."

"Holy…."

"That first night we met, when I whooped for joy, was because I'd just got the news that the police had cleared me of any wrongdoing. And then, just last night, I learned that the medical board decided not to take my license."

He stared at her, searching her eyes. "All of that kind of makes me want to track him down and kick his ass."

"He's going to prison. His sentencing is right after the holidays. And I'm fine, so—"

"Are you? Did you lose your job over it?"

She nodded. "It was an elite hospital. I don't blame them." Smiling across the table she said, "And I'm fine, and I'm here, and it's not a fun thing to talk about at a Christmas ball. Finish your food so we can dance again. And um… let's attack one of those dessert tables."

He nodded. "Your wish is my command."

It was just the dim lighting, or maybe it was the country band, playing holiday songs in a slow, sultry cadence that lovers could dance to. It was the dress she wore, or maybe the shoes, or maybe the way that Santa pendant rested right at the v of her cleavage and kept drawing his eye. Or maybe it was her eyes, the way they sparkled in the spinning red and green lights, or the sound of her laugh or the way her smile reached her entire face.

Maybe it was just her.

Whatever it was, something was happening to him. He was feeling kind of light headed, and not from Grandma Betty's spiced rum. It was like he was under a spell. A charm. Entranced.

By her.

They ate, and they drank. They danced, and each time it felt a little more natural to press their bodies close, so they were touching from head to thigh, while they moved around the floor.

Then it happened. They were dancing off their dessert, and he lowered his head just at the same moment she was lifting hers, and their lips just sort of found each other. It was long, and slow, and oh so sexy.

Then the lights came up. He'd had no idea how much time had passed. But the band was finished, and the ball, at an end. He held her close beside him as they went back to their table, gathered up their things and headed out to the truck to take her home.

His home, he hoped. His room, above the Long Branch. His bed, where she would spend the whole night in his arms.

He helped her into the truck and got behind the wheel, and then he drove them back to Big Falls. As they neared the village, she was snuggled close to him on the seat and he had one arm around her shoulders.

He slowed down as they neared the Long Branch. She lifted her head, pressed her lips to his cheek, and said, "Tonight was wonderful. But it's too soon for more. Right now, I mean."

"I wasn't going to ask," he said. Because he had sure been hoping she'd offer.

"It's just...he burned me pretty badly, Darryl. He betrayed

me. I'm having a hard time trusting again, and I still don't know all that much about you."

"I'm looking forward to changing that." He drove on past the saloon, but didn't pick up speed. "One thing you should know about me is that I haven't celebrated Christmas in a very long time. And there isn't much that I thought could budge me from that habit. But tonight, I had a really fantastic time. I didn't even mind the holiday music and all the twinkling lights."

They were passing through the village and then drove out the far end, toward Vidalia and Bobby Joe's place. When they got there, he got out and came around to help her down, only to find she'd already shucked the shoes. She hopped down easily on her own, landing on his toes and in his arms.

"I had a wonderful time too, Darryl. Thank you." She fingered the pendant. "For everything." Then she stood on tiptoe, and pressed her lips to his.

He wrapped her up tight, and kissed her back, long and slow. She tasted like spiced rum, only way more intoxicating.

"Goodnight, Darryl," she said. Then she hurried to the front door, and was gone behind it before he could even clear his vision.

"'Night, Sophie," he muttered. Then he walked back to his truck, shaking his head, and feeling as surprised as if a lobster had just crawled out of his ear as it dawned on him very clearly, that Sophie wasn't just a holiday fling. He had *feelings* for her bubbling up all over the place.

This could *be* something. Something he hadn't even thought he wanted up to now. Up to the first time he'd set eyes on her, really.

Just about the same amount of time he'd been lying to her.

CHAPTER EIGHT

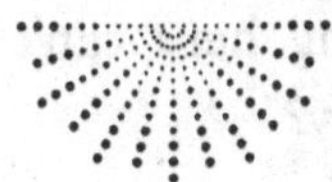

When local bakery owner Sunny smiled at her from across the counter the next morning, Sophia thought there should be angels singing backup. "Hey, you're Vidalia's new niece, aren't you?"

"I didn't realize I'd been here long enough to be famous already," she said, extending a hand. "Sophia McIntyre."

"Sunny Jones," Sunny replied. "So what do you think of Big Falls, Sophie?"

Sophia bit her lip for a second to keep from correcting her on the nickname and answered her, glad to be distracted from worrying about whether she should sleep with Darryl Champlain or not.

She wanted to.

But should she?

Right, conversation. Distraction. What was the question again? Right, got it.

"I love it, here. I grew up near here, you know. Well, fifty miles away. My family moved when I was still in elementary school."

"And your uncle Bobby Joe had a history here. I'm glad he

came back. He's the best thing to happen to this town in a long time. That's the consensus among the gossips, anyway."

"Odd he ended up back here though."

"And now you're here, too," Sunny said. "They say this town chooses her residents. You know that?"

Sophia looked at her, brows raised, almost perking her ears to hear more.

"The ones who belong here can't seem to leave. So how about you? You gonna stay?"

She opened her mouth to say no, but found the word didn't want to come out. She laughed at herself for wondering if some force was preventing it.

"I didn't mean to pry," Sunny said quickly, mistaking her long silence for unwillingness to answer. "Who'd want to stay here anyway? It's gonna be miserable, having to go all the way to Tucker Lake for everything from ulcers to typhus."

"Ulcers to...what now?" Some of the small town Oklahoma euphemisms had come right back to her, but as far as Sophia knew, she'd never heard that one before.

"You haven't heard? Doc is quitting and moving to Boca. Some big retirement community with golf carts and swimming pools. Just like that." She snapped her fingers. "Well, he *is* seventy-three, but—I'm sorry, Sophie. Didn't mean to go off like that. What can I get for you?"

Sophia stood there a minute, her brain spewing a dozen reasons why a perfect stranger would just happen to mention that the local doctor was leaving the town in a lurch. But for the life of her she couldn't think of one.

Other than her letter to Santa, at least.

It felt good to think that. It surprised her how good it felt. Kind of innocent. She felt like she'd felt as a little girl who'd believed in Santa Claus like she believed in her own mamma. She'd been that little girl. Maybe...maybe she wanted to believe in something again.

Sunny was smiling, waiting for her to place her order. Sophia blinked out of what could only be described as a blinding rush of Christmas spirit—and said, "Right. A dozen half-moons, please. I've got inventory today and I want to bribe people to help me."

"I'll throw in a couple of extras, then." Sunny opened a glass case and used tongs to load the cookies into a wax paper-lined, pink cardboard box. She closed the lid and used a couple of pieces of masking tape to seal it. Then she pulled off her gloves and punched a few buttons on the oversized antique cash register.

Sophia paid in cash and told Sunny to keep the change. Then she walked out of the bakery, blinking slowly and wondering if what she thought had happened, had actually happened.

Was this a sign? Was this her answer?

Man, if the local Santa was as good as she was starting to think he was, the children of Big Falls were in for one heck of a Christmas!

Sophia wrestled with her decision all the way back to the Long Branch. She was so wound up, she had barely slept all night long, and when she had, the dreams had been….

She closed her eyes and a shiver ran up her spine.

She was a single, adult woman. A doctor. She wanted to have sex with a willing, gorgeous, funny, smart hunk who danced like a god, and smelled even better.

So she was going to.

She had a key to the Long Branch. Her cousins wanted her to have access to the place at all times. Hell, they'd wanted her to use one of the rooms upstairs, but she'd refused. Working for the boys was enough. She didn't want to live with them too.

But having that key sure did make for easy access.

She parked her car around back, disappointed that Darryl's wasn't there. Didn't matter. He couldn't have gone far. She could text him, tell him to come back to his room, ASAP.

She smiled, imagining how he'd react to that. And how fast he could get there. It had *better* be fast, or she might chicken out.

She let herself in through the kitchen. "Hello? Anyone here?"

But her own voice just echoed back at her.

She headed through the kitchen and into the bar, her shoes clicking on the hardwood. It smelled like that orange scented oil they used on every inch of hardwood in the place until she got deeper into the place and the smell of the Christmas tree took over.

She peeked into the dining room, but it was empty. Joey and Robert had rooms upstairs, but their SUVs weren't there. Jason was probably at that place he'd rented. Vidalia said it was an old blacksmith's shop that had been closed down for a hundred years. No one knew what the heck Jason McIntyre wanted with the broken-down old place, and when asked, he usually muttered something about it being historic and changed the subject.

The cousins were seldom at the saloon during the mornings, because their new stepmother Vidalia and the family that came with her, tended to keep them pretty busy.

Vidalia's five daughters, their husbands and their kids were a big noisy welcoming brood and they would wrap Sophia right up in their cocoon if they could. She'd been in town long enough to share one Sunday dinner with the bunch so far. It had felt a little bit uncomfortable to be surrounded by so many people who wanted to be family, but weren't really.

And yet the more time she spent with them, the more it felt as if maybe they could be.

She went into Jason's unlocked office, took the keyring right off the rack, and then she headed upstairs and rapped on Joey's door, just to be sure. No answer. Then she tried Robert's. Nothing. Okay, good. The place was empty.

She headed to the remaining guest room, the one the boys had wanted her to use, and tried a key. Then another. The third one fit.

Biting her lip and telling herself she wasn't committing too terrible a sin, she unlocked Darryl Champlain's door and tiptoed inside.

The room was simple and clean. Beige carpet, nice and thick. King size bed, sort of made up, and there were clothes on the floor. The bathroom door was closed. There were two nightstands, one on either side of the bed, and one of them had a photograph of her on it. Not in a frame or anything, just lying there on top of a file folder.

Everything in Sophia went cold. What the hell did this mean?

She turned a slow circle, scanning the room, looking for something, anything to tell her what was going on here. Why would he have a picture of her?

Unless he was working for Skyler.

Her spinal fluid iced over. Keys and a wallet lay on top of a nightstand, along with that badge holder she'd already seen. The one with his Secret Service badge and ID. She picked up the wallet, not the badge one, but the regular one, thinking that would be the best place to find out what he was really up to.

And then she froze, holding it in her hands, open, as her brain finally asked her how his wallet could be here if he wasn't.

And suddenly the closed bathroom door opened, and he stepped out wearing nothing but a towel. He looked at her, and his brows bunched. "What are you doing in my room, Sophie?"

She couldn't look at him. It hurt to look at him, so she lowered her eyes and they fell on the open wallet in her hand, and on the ID card inside it. *Darryl Champlain, Licensed Private Investigator, Private Security Services.*

She lifted her head again. "What are you doing in my *life*, Darryl?" She tossed the wallet onto the bed. "I'll tell you what, Mr. Private Eye, I'll give you 'til the end of the day to get out of town. You stick around here any longer and your ass is going to be very, *very* sorry."

She lurched toward the door, but he stepped right into her path and said, "It's not what you think."

"No? You're not spying on me for pay?"

He tipped his head to one side just a little. "Well, yeah, but—"

"Get out of my way."

"Sophie, just wait, just gimme three seconds." He closed his hands around her shoulders as he said it. They were warm and they felt good. And she was so damn disappointed she was on the edge of tears. All this letter to Santa baloney had made her hope—more than hope, it had made her believe... She'd been cleared legally. Her medical license was safe. She'd been vindicated. And now there was a glimmer of potential about her life's work, too. A way she might be able to keep doing what she loved right here in the town she had somehow also started to love.

She'd started to think maybe Darryl was...the one. Yeah, she'd let herself get a little bit carried away with the whole believing in Santa Claus thing, hadn't she?

Darryl's big hands as they slid down her arms and closed around hers. Her eyes followed—big mistake because that meant looking at his all but naked body. His chest was so smooth and hard that her hands were aching to run across it. And the way that towel was hitched over one hip and slung low across the other made her want to reach up and yank it away.

He let go of her hands, and damning herself for being an idiot, she pressed them to his chest. She couldn't help herself.

He stood stock still for just a second, waiting. She was waiting too, mainly to see if she had the strength to walk away. But she didn't. Hell, she didn't want to turn away. She moved her palms over his skin, and his arms curled around her, pulled her body to his. She felt the bulge behind the towel and closed her eyes in delicious longing. It had been a long time.

He closed his hands on her shoulders. "Please let me explain?" he asked softly, his voice as raspy as his still-unshaven face.

She lifted her head, stared into his eyes, saw the desire burning there, and felt a rush of feminine power. "Not right now," she said. "Just kiss me."

So he did. Only, not the way she'd expected him to. He slid one hand around to her nape, and slowly threaded his fingers up into her hair, sending chills and shivers all the way down her spine. Then he slid the other hand around her waist, inching his way to the small of her back to urge her a little bit closer. He lowered his head slowly, so slowly she ached for him to hurry. His eyes held hers until she closed them. And then, finally, he touched his soft, soft lips to hers, and her bones melted. He moved them, gently, softly, capturing, suckling, releasing, over and over. And then he lifted his head away, took two steps backward, and stood there. "Not until you let me explain."

Sophia felt ridiculously cold now that his arms were no longer around her. She shivered, and that seemed to snap her out of the spell.

She opened her mouth, but couldn't speak, didn't know what to say. She didn't want to hear that he was working for Skyler. And she didn't want to hear him lie to her. She just wanted him.

She picked up the pieces of her dignity, turned and walked out of the room, pulling the door closed behind her.

And then she ran the rest of the way down the stairs, out through the kitchen to her car, jumped in and sped away. The cookies were still on the passenger seat. And inventory was going to have to wait.

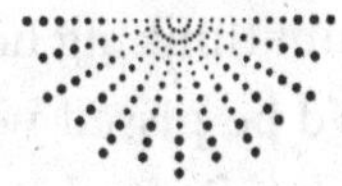

CHAPTER NINE

Her cell phone was ringing before she even made it home, despite that it was only a ten-minute drive. She checked it before answering of course, in case it was Darryl.

It wasn't. It was Vidalia. She was too nice a person to be sent to voicemail, so Sophia picked up the phone and said hello.

"I'm so glad you're there, Sophie. I've been worrying about you. I was calling because I want to make sure you'll be home for Sunday dinner. It's the last one before Christmas. Family should be together."

She smiled. She'd been longing for a family to spend Christmas with ever since her own mom had passed away three years ago and her dad only a few months later. That was love, what they had. So why was she resisting the open arms of this newly enlarged branch of her family?

That, she thought, bore some consideration. But in the meantime, she decided to open her heart. "Of course I'll be there. Can I bring anything?"

"I am never opposed to an additional dessert," she said. "But don't fuss."

She glanced at the seat. "How do half moon cookies sound?"

"Well, they sound fine, as long as there are two dozen or so."

"I'm halfway there."

"Wonderful."

~

Darryl's head hadn't stopped spinning since he'd watched Sophie walk out of his room thinking he'd betrayed her.

Dammit, he knew she'd be pissed when she found out what he'd been up to, but he hadn't figured on this. What the *hell*?

Okay, okay, he had to remember the point here. He put on his clothes as he reminded himself she wasn't entirely the injured party here. She broke into his room, went through his stuff.

He'd awoken with a slight headache from "Grandma Betty's" spiced rum punch, and had decided to soak in the big old claw-footed tub in his bathroom, and he fell asleep in the water. Fell asleep...thinking about her, actually.

He'd dropped his truck at Armstrong's Garage last night after their date, for a quick oil change. The owner was yet another of his bosses' relatives. He'd walked back from the garage to his room above the Long Branch. It wasn't that far, and it was a nice night, for December. And besides all that, he was thinking it would serve the same purpose a cold shower would've done, because his night with Sophie had left him more wound up than a billy goat on the fourth of July.

There was a tap on his door. He was buttoning his shirt and decided to stop, just in case it was her again.

Idiot. He was an idiot. Why was he hoping it was Sophie? Why was he leaving his shirt unbuttoned in case it was? She thought he was working for her sleaze bag ex. She oughtta know better than that.

He opened the door, saw Jason McIntyre standing on the other side, and resumed buttoning. He ignored the disappointment that rushed through him at the sight of his boss. "Morning, Jason."

"Morning Darryl. Um, I hate to ask you this and please don't take it wrong, but I uh…." He shifted his feet and didn't quite meet Darryl's eyes.

"What's up, boss? Just spill it."

"My keys are missing," Jason blurted.

"Your keys?"

"Yeah. The keys to every room in this building. I left them in my office, like always, and–"

Darryl held up a hand. "That would explain why I found your cousin in my room when I got out of the bathtub just now."

Jason blinked. "Sophia?"

"Yeah."

"What the hell? Where does she get off taking my keys and–"

"She must've um…been suspicious of me. Yeah, that's probably it. I must've slipped last night, somehow."

"At the Haggerty House Ball with her?" Jason's his voice low.

"Hootenanny," he corrected. "And it doesn't matter. She knows I'm a PI, and she saw that photo you guys sent me so I'd know her when I saw her."

Jason was still staring, waiting. After a long moment he heaved a sigh. "What's going on with you and her?"

"It's nothing." Darryl turned around to walk to his dresser for a clean pair of socks and to avoid Jason's increasingly curious eyes. "We shared a booth at the diner yesterday morning. No big deal."

"So you had breakfast together."

"Yeah."

"And then you took her to the ball. Excuse me. Hootenanny."

"The tickets were an early Christmas gift from your local Santa. She opened it while we were having breakfast. I just happened to be there. I think she'd have asked anyone who had been there with her instead of me."

He glanced at his wallet, still lying on the bed, picked it up. "She saw my PI license."

"Sounds like that's not all she saw."

Darryl snapped his head up fast. "What the hell is that supposed to mean?"

"You said you were in the tub. Did you walk out here buck naked and give her the full show, or what?"

"No. I didn't. And if I had, it wouldn't have been my fault. My door was closed and locked."

"Yeah. Okay."

"I didn't do anything inappropriate here." Yeah, he did. He totally did. He kissed his boss's cousin, and almost more than kissed. She was the subject of a job. Bad form. Real bad.

"Did you tell her why we really hired you?"

"No. I was kind of hoping you'd do that."

"Why would I?"

"Because it's unethical for me to do it, and because I don't want her thinking I work for her piece-of-crap ex, that's why."

"Why do you care what she thinks?"

"I don't." Why the hell did he avert his eyes when he said it? "But she's going to rat me out to you and she'll expect you to send me packing. You're gonna have to tell her something."

"We'll see." Jason lowered his head, shook it, and said, "My father wants you at Sunday dinner tomorrow, out at his place."

"Your father?" The total change of topics had his head spinning all over again. "But I haven't even met him."

"Wouldn't matter. He and Vidalia aren't very good at taking no for an answer. We gather around two."

"Tomorrow at two. Gotcha. I'll...be there."

"Good."

Darryl blurted, "Will um...will Sophie be there?"

Jason looked at him, crooked one eyebrow.

"Just because...you know, it might be awkward, if she still thinks I'm working for the bad guy."

Jason, who clearly saw right through him, nodded. "She'll be there."

~

Saturday nights were the busiest nights of the week at the Long Branch. The tourists who were the lifeblood of the business came all week long. When you're on vacation, every day is Saturday, or you're not doing it right. But on true Saturday nights, a lot of the locals were looking for a good time, too. The local dive-bar, the OK Corral, was owned by Vidalia herself, giving the recently formed Brand-McIntyre clan kind of an unfair corner on the market, if you asked Sophia, but no one was asking. And they were good people, all of them. You didn't have to know them very long to know that. No one in town seemed to be complaining about the Brand-McIntyre saloon monopoly.

Despite their loyalty to their local hangout though, people liked to mix it up once in a while, and Saturday nights were the time they loved doing it best. For that reason, the boys had decided to skip the dinner theater bit they had going—re-enactments of scenes from the old TV series *Gunsmoke* mostly. That was for tourists. Starting last summer, Saturday nights at the Long Branch included live music by country bands, locals and now and then some real up-and-comers. The band setting up equipment now, were one of the most popular in the area, according to Joey.

"Hey," Darryl said.

She'd known he was there before he'd said a word. It was early yet. The customers were only just beginning to wander in. She looked at him, but didn't say anything. She couldn't believe she'd kissed him like that—and would've done more than kissed him—even though he was probably working for Skyler.

"Who's the band?" he asked, sliding onto a barstool in front of her.

She'd been pouring nearly empty bottles together to make room for more full ones on the rack. Bourbon, right now. The good stuff. She set the bottle down so she wouldn't get distracted by his eyes and spill it.

"Rising Outlaw," Sophia said. "I wonder if they really meant Rising Outlaws and just ran out of room on the drum." She looked at him, saw him frowning at her like he was trying to figure her out and shrugged. "What? I think about things like that."

"You have a curious mind." He leaned his elbows on the bar so he could pull himself closer, and whispered, "That why you were going through my wallet?"

"I was going through your wallet to find out why you had a photo of me on your nightstand."

"So then why were you in my room in the first place?"

She looked at him, closed her eyes and looked away, angry at the heat that spread through her cheeks.

"Hell, hell, hell," he muttered. Then he took a deep breath and said, "Screw professional ethics. I'm here because your cousins hired me to keep an eye on you. They didn't tell me anything except that you had an ex who wasn't taking the break up well and had tried to kick your door in before you left town to come back here."

"My cousins?" Her jaw wouldn't close for a second to form another word. Then it did, and she clenched it and tried really hard to be angry instead of relieved. "Those overbearing, over-protective, meddling *jerks*!"

"They care about you."

"I guess." Sighing heavily, she finished pouring one bourbon into the other, capped the full one, and wiped both bottles down.

"I didn't know you were a doctor until you told me," Darryl said. "A doctor. Damn, Sophie, I'm not sure I'm good enough for you."

He leaned over the bar, giving a quick look behind them before stroking the back of her hand. It sent a warm feeling up her arm. "So how is it you know your way around the backside of a bar so darn well?"

"I bartended my way through med-school, usually at one of the places Uncle Bobby Joe had his hands in. He made his fortune finding failing bars and clubs, fixing them up and flipping them. Till he came here and decided to stay."

"I'm impressed."

"He's an impressive man."

"I'm impressed by you. Bartending your way through school. That's something."

She shrugged. "It's not as impressive as the Secret Service," she said. "Was that true?"

He nodded. "I never lied to you."

Why was she starting to feel a little bit giddy that he wasn't working for her ex after all? It took a minute for the anger to drain, but once it did, the relief was almost buoyant. He was working for her cousins. Watching out for her. It offended her feminist sensibilities, and yet reassured her about the magic currently unfolding in her life. With him.

That Santa Claus might've been onto something after all. Then again, Darryl was planning to leave here and head back to his old life pretty soon. So there was still that.

"I'm sorry I started us off by lying to you," he said. "I wasn't expecting this….whatever it is between us. I wasn't ready for it. I didn't handle it right. But I promise, I'm never gonna be less than honest with you again."

"Wow." She just blinked at him, almost wondering if he could truly be real.

"And I'm sorry you went through all that crap with Skyler, and the police and losing your job."

She was quiet for a moment. "All things considered, everything worked out in my favor. But Skyler seems to be having a hard time letting go."

"Of you?" he asked.

Wow, his eyes were intense right then. "Yeah. And he's walking around free until his sentencing."

"Are you afraid of him?"

"Not in the least," she said, looking him right in the eye again. "I could kick his ass one-handed, especially when he's falling down drunk, which he's been most of the time since this all came out." She shook her head. "That's what the boys don't get. At heart, Skyler's a marshmallow. He wouldn't hurt a fly. I just needed to get someplace where I could sleep at night and… and…" She sighed. "And try to figure things out. You know, why all this happened, what it means."

"Does it have to mean something?" he asked, frowning a little, like he really wanted to know.

At some point she had leaned her elbows on the bar, too, and her face had made its way awfully close to his. She backed away, straightened up. "I didn't used to think so. But since I've been here…I'm not sure. Maybe *everything* means something," she said. Then she shrugged and turned to put the full bourbon bottle onto the rack behind her. "Another couple of months, and my prescription pad would've been obsolete. We were in the process of switching over to an entirely computerized system. Ironic, right?"

"That stinks, Sophie. I'm sorry it happened." He straightened up as well, set himself back on his stool.

"I'm not sorry it happened. Now that I really think about it, I'm not sorry at all." She reached for a tall glass, poured him a sweet tea and set it on a coaster in front of him. "I was at first, but I gotta tell you, this 'everything-happens-for-a-reason thing' is starting to make sense to me. I'm starting to feel excited to see what the reason was for this. This whole thing woke me up, Darryl. It showed me I was in the wrong relationship with the wrong guy, and apparently in the wrong city, in the wrong state, working in the wrong job." She bit her lower lip, then said, "I knew it, too. I knew it way down deep. I'd been feeling restless and grouchy and tense. I just couldn't put my finger on why. But that was why. I ignored my feelings until the problem got so big I had no choice but to make a change."

He was staring at her as if he'd never seen her before. "That's... a little too deep for me."

She shrugged. "Yeah. Was for me too, when I first heard it."

"Who'd you hear it from?" he asked.

She smiled and recalled that twinkle in Santa's eye. "Santa Claus." Then she noticed Rising Outlaw's lead singer, Ben Armstrong, waving at her from the stage. The band was ready. She gave him a nod. "Got a surprise for you, Darryl."

Frowning, Darryl spun his barstool slowly around as the band played the opening chords of "Christmas Blues," his one and only hit song, and Sophia prepared to see a smile on his face.

He slid off his stool to stand up on his feet. She was still speaking to his back and couldn't see his reaction. "I thought I'd have Jason introduce you after they play it. You can take a little bow. You okay with that?"

"No," he said.

Sophia stiffened. The word was clipped and kind of gravelly.

"No, I'm not okay with that." He walked away, across the floor and through the batwing doors. They flapped three times after he'd passed.

Oh, hell. She'd really messed up, then, hadn't she?

She couldn't help but wonder how and why.

CHAPTER TEN

*I*t was the damn song.

He'd been doing great, having fun, starting to get into the whole holiday thing for the first time in recent memory. Every shop had carols playing, bells jingling. Every day the church bells rang with a song at high noon. He knew the lineup by heart. "Silent Night," "The Carol of the Bells," and "Away in a Manger." The entire saloon was decked to high heaven and so was the whole danged town.

He had not thought, when he'd accepted the job offer via the net, and headed out here, that he was moving into Christmas central.

And yet, somehow it had been all right. Being with Sophie had made it all right.

Until they had to go and play that damned song.

He probably owed Sophie an apology for reacting to it the way he had. She'd just tried to do something nice for him.

Sophie. The thought of her hit the brakes on his racing thoughts. Her face hovered in his mind's eye, and he relived those moments in his bedroom upstairs. That kiss. Holy Moses. And she'd been there for that. For him.

She was smart. A doctor, for crying out loud. He didn't think of himself as an intellectual, really. He'd been a good soldier right up until he'd got himself blown up, and then after he'd recovered, he'd been a good cop, and later a good agent. Right now, he was a good PI-slash-bodyguard. He didn't know if that was going to be forever, but he didn't think so.

She was quirky, looking for reasons for everything, the way she was. Deep. Kind of spiritual. He liked it. He found that knowing it made him like her even more than he had before.

He was walking around outside the saloon. He'd gone out through the front doors, not the back, and he could see the parking lot was almost filled to capacity. He was on the job and shouldn't shirk his duties, even if they weren't the reason he'd truly been hired.

But he needed a break.

Thrusting his hands into his pockets, he paced past the parking lot and walked out into the grassy meadow beside it. The din of the band—which had wrapped up his song and started another—was almost non-existent there. The stars were blinking to life in the dark blue sky. The sun hadn't been down long. It wasn't full dark yet, but the air was cool enough that he could see his breath.

It cleared his head both literally and figuratively. Yeah. Okay, so he and Sophie had got off on the wrong foot. He hadn't been honest with her, and she'd thought the worst. But things were out in the open now. Things were better now.

He didn't know exactly what "things" he was referring to. He just knew he liked her. He liked her a lot.

But he didn't think that "everything-happens-for-a-reason" bit was very logical. He'd almost been a father once. A teenage father, but a father, all the same. That had been taken away from him, and an IED had ensured the chance would never come again. He couldn't for the life of him think of any *reason* for something like that.

He took one more breath of brisk fresh air, and thrusting his hands into his jeans' pockets, started back. He didn't know why he still let his oldest heartbreak get to him the way he did. He was usually fine, just...all this freaking Christmas. Man. It brought it all back.

He was almost to the door when he saw the guy in the hoodie. Same blue hoody underneath the same denim jacket. Same hunched-up posture. He was probably six two and skinny, and he was lurking around outside the saloon. Not on his way in or out, just hanging.

Darryl headed that way. "Hey. What are you doing out here?"

The guy jerked his head Darryl's way and then took off at a run. That got Darryl's blood pumping and he ran after him, vaguely aware of footsteps behind him. Then Sophie yelled, "Darryl, no. Leave him alone, he's fine."

He caught the guy by one shoulder, yanked him around so hard, he stumbled and fell on his ass. Then the stranger looked up at him, his hood falling back as he did. A shock of dark hair fell over his face, covering one eye. He was a kid. Just a kid.

Sophia grabbed his arm and yanked it away. "What do you think you're doing, Darryl? Let him be!" Then she moved him out of the way, wedging herself between him and the kid, and reached down for the boy's hand, helped him get up. "You okay? Did he hurt you?"

"I'm all right."

The kid stood there in the glow of the parking lot lights. He had dark, thick lashes, midnight blue eyes, and a narrow face with cheekbones sculpted by a master. His expressive eyes darted from Sophia to Darryl and back again. He looked scared.

Darryl sighed. "This is the third time I've seen you lurking around this saloon, kid. What are you up to?"

"Nothing," he muttered, straightening his jacket around him and hunching into it. He couldn't hold Darryl's gaze.

"What's your name?"

"None of your business. I was stupid to ever come here." He shook his head, then just turned and took off running like an Olympic sprinter, and when Darryl lunged as if to go after him, Sophie stepped right in front of him so fast he bumped into her and caught her shoulders to keep one or both of them from falling over.

"Sophie, come on. He's up to no good."

"He's a kid and he's in trouble. Geeze, that's the same one who was sleeping on the bench under the town Christmas tree, Darryl. How can you be so heartless?"

She gazed down the road where the kid had been swallowed up by the shadows. "I wanted to help him, but you scared him off, you bully."

"Just a damn second here," he said, blurting the words as fast as they came. They were almost blurting themselves. "I show up and you're suspicious I'm working for your drug dealer fiancé–"

"Ex-fiancé!"

"—and *he* shows up, starts lurking around everywhere you happen to be, and you want to *help him*?"

"He's a child, Darryl."

"He's six-two, Sophie."

She made a noise like she had a hunk of meat caught in her throat, spun on her heel and stomped back inside. "Come on," she said. "We're going to put a stop to this crap right now." She strode across the parking lot, and after one last look in the direction the kid had fled, he followed. She marched through the outer doors and then through the batwings like a hurricane, then stomped through the entire saloon, catching each McIntyre cousin's eye on the way.

She didn't have to say anything. The fire in her gaze was enough. They all fell into the comet's tail she was creating behind her. Her trajectory took them into Jason's office, which wasn't really built to house five.

"Close the door, Joey," she said.

Joey closed it, looking from one of his brothers to the other. "Oh, hell. She knows, doesn't she?"

"Looks that way," Jason said, sending an angry glare at Darryl.

"I had to tell her. She thought I was working for the ex," Darryl explained.

"What is it to you, what she thought?" Rob demanded.

Sophie hooked her pinkie fingers into her lips and gave a whistle that might've made their ears bleed. Darryl was tempted to check.

Everyone went silent and she said, "Now, be quiet and just listen. I came out here to get away from a controlling, secret-keeping man, and apparently, I landed myself right in the middle of a whole flock of them. I do not need protecting from wimpy, drunk-ass Skyler, and I certainly don't need protecting from a poor, hungry, homeless teenage boy."

"What teenage boy?" Jason asked. "There's a hungry homeless boy in the mix someplace?"

"The hoody-wearing stalker," Darryl explained.

She turned to face Jason. "Tell Darryl he's fired, or I go back to your dad's, pack my bags and head to New York."

"Sophia—"

"Right after I tell Vidalia what you three did," she added.

Jason tried to stay stoic, but Joey went kind of pale and started talking rapidly. "Look, okay, we get it. You're a grownup and you don't need protecting. But it turns out, we *do* need a bouncer."

"Head of security," Jason corrected.

"Joey's right," Rob said. "We do need him." Then he shifted his gaze to the man in question. "Darryl, your services to watch over our cousin are no longer needed. We'll cash out on that before closing time, pay you what we owe—"

"I broke the contract by telling her the truth. I can't take any money for that," Darryl said.

The boys all exchanged a look that Sophia thought indicated respect for that decision. And then Jason said, "But we'd like to keep you on as head of security for as long as you'd like to stay in town."

Darryl heaved a sigh. "I don't know, guys."

"Well, you gotta give us time to find a replacement at least," Joey said. "Two weeks notice is the custom, isn't it?"

"Not for a fake job."

"It's *not* a fake job," Jason said. "We've got the paperwork. You signed on. You agreed to the terms."

Sophia frowned at Jason and wanted to throttle him. Yes, she'd been holding her breath and willing Darryl to say he wanted to stay, but she wanted it to be *his* decision. And her cousins were twisting his arm.

And now he was looking at her as if for the answer. She wanted *him* to decide to stay, darn it all! Shrugging as if she didn't care one way or the other, she said, "Stay on if you want, Darryl. But no more watching over me. And that goes for all of you. Got it?"

"Got it." The three McIntyres said it in unison, and Sophie stared at Darryl, awaiting his agreement.

"Yeah. I've got it," he said.

She nodded, turned and walked out of the office and back to the bar.

Darryl eyed the three brothers. "Guys, this kid she's defending is almost a man, sixteen, maybe seventeen. Tall, skinny, wearing a blue hoodie and denim jacket—"

"I *have* noticed him hanging around," Jason said.

Darryl nodded. "Yeah. Around Sophie. And I don't like it."

"Neither do I," Jason said. "He might be working for her ex. And no matter what she says, that guy was bad news."

"Most drug dealers are. You roll around with dogs, you're gonna get fleas. I'd like to check this kid out," Darryl said. "With your permission."

Jason looked at his brothers. Joey grimaced and shook his head, and Rob just lowered his. "I think we'd best respect her wishes," Jason said.

Darryl heaved a sigh. "Okay. All right. Still, I'm going to take you up on your offer to hang around a while longer. I'll feel better if I do."

"So…this is your two weeks' notice?" Robert asked.

"Yeah, I guess it is."

He was going to check the kid out on his own. Just in case. Because he'd seen men like the one Sophie's ex before. Obsessed, controlling, incapable of letting go. What did she think good old Skyler would have done if he'd managed to kick her door in one of those times when he'd tried? She wasn't afraid of him, she said. His gut told him that she should be.

And something inside him wouldn't let him leave until he'd made damn sure she was safe.

CHAPTER ELEVEN

On Sunday afternoon, the Brand family farmhouse just outside of Big Falls, was busting at the seams with family.

It was Sophia's second Sunday dinner with the Brand-McIntyre clan, but this one was even noisier and more boisterous than the first had been—probably because it was so close to Christmas. The excitement of the coming big day was palpable.

She was sipping eggnog with her uncle in front of the twinkling tree, her stomach growling because of the smells wafting in from the kitchen.

"This is a huge family you've married into, Uncle Bobby Joe," she said, stating the obvious. "And your own boys aren't even here yet."

"They generally show up right before we sit down to eat, and spend the time in between asking when dinner will be ready," he said. "This, despite that it's always on the table at five, no matter what. My beautiful bride is adamant about Sunday dinners." He looked at the tree, shook his head wistfully. "Especially at this time of year."

She nodded and found a comfy spot near the tree. Its multicolored lights were flashing and sparkling beneath hundreds of ornaments, most of them homemade. She could barely see the needled boughs. Tiny hands had created countless decorations over decades, she could tell just by looking. Glittery pinecones and paper snowflakes and popsicle stick sleds painted red, and lots more.

"How are you, darlin'?" Bobby Joe asked. And he made it a serious question.

She thought about her answer before she gave it, instead of blurting the usual "fine, and you?" She considered for a long moment, then nodded. "Actually, I'm good. Way better than I was when I got here. And I think, getting better all the time."

"Then why are you looking a little misty-eyed?"

She shrugged but moved nearer the tree. "Just realizing how much I've missed having family around me at Christmas time," she said. "I didn't realize how much I wanted this sort of thing. Or maybe I just told myself I didn't miss it, so I'd feel better after Mom and Dad passed. I've cut loose a lot of ballast in the past few weeks. A job that wasn't right for me, a relationship that couldn't have been more wrong. I'm drifting a little now, and only just realizing that I'm looking for the perfect port."

"That," said Vidalia from behind her, "is just about the best place to be. Nothing but potential. Don't you think, Darryl?"

Darryl? Sophie turned around, trying not to look too urgent about it, and there he was, the gorgeous cop turned PI turned fake bouncer, standing just behind Vidalia's shoulder.

"I've been drifting a little bit myself lately," he said.

"Well, if it's a home port you're wanting, you won't find one better than Big Falls," Vidalia declared with a grin. "Especially at Christmastime. Will they, Bobby Joe?"

"Nope," he agreed. "This family has to be the most Christmassy bunch I've ever come across."

"With good reason." Vidalia moved up beside her husband and into the circle of his arm. "We have a pretty regular tradition of Christmas miracles in this family, in case you haven't noticed."

Other family members were crowding into the living room: Kara Brand with her husband, local cop Jimmy Corona and ten-year-old Tyler, Maya and her husband Caleb, each holding the hand of one of their four-year-old twins, Dahlia and Cal.

"Big Falls is full of magic at Christmastime, that's for sure," said Selene, Vidalia's youngest, who was also half sister to Jason, Robert and Joey, and therefore, Sophia's cousin.

Sophia tilted her head to one side. "I've been experiencing a little bit of that since I've been here. Just one problem after another seems to be…falling away."

"You write that letter to Santa?" Vidalia asked, which made Sophia glance at the mantel, where Aunt Vidalia's own Dear Santa letter still lay, and then at Darryl, who seemed to be waiting for her reply.

"I did," she said. "I met him my first day in town, you know. The Big Falls Santa."

"He's the best," young Tyler said. When I first came here, I was just little. I told him what I wanted for Christmas, and I got it." As he said it, he sent a look full of love at Kara, his adopted mom.

"I got my twins on Christmas Eve," Maya said, "Right upstairs, in the middle of a freak storm. And Caleb even managed to get to my side in time."

"And I got a daughter I didn't know I had," Uncle Bobby Joe said with a loving look Selene's way, "and a new lease on life when I was right at death's door." He dropped a kiss on the top of Vidalia's raven hair. "Yep, this place is magic all right. Or maybe it's just this family."

"What did you ask Santa for, Sophie?" asked one of Maya's twins, Dahlia.

She smiled at the little girl, thinking of all the things she'd written in her letter. She'd been cleared of any crime. Her license to practice medicine was safe and sound. She was sleeping at night, peacefully and soundly. And most recently, she'd picked up a clue as to how she could do what she loved best in the place she now thought she wanted to stay. All that remained on her wish list was true love.

She glanced at Darryl as she thought it, then looked away quickly when she found him gazing back at her with some kind of question in his eyes.

"Sometimes, Dahlia, people don't want to tell their wishes," Maya told her little girl.

Dahlia nodded sagely and said, "I guess that's okay, as long as you told Santa."

"I did," Sophie said.

Then the little girl ran over to her, holding out her hand. "Want to go swing in the backyard?"

"Sure."

"Yay! Come on, Cal!," she called to her twin brother, who didn't argue. "You, too Tyler!" Then she pointed right at Darryl. "And you, too, new guy! Come on, let's go." She smiled at her grandmother, who gave her an approving nod as if to say, "Well done."

~

It was a gorgeous afternoon, chilly enough so you could see your breath, but sunny and bright. Sophia was glad she hadn't taken her jacket off. Darryl closed the back door and crossed the snow-dusted lawn toward the massive wooden play set where the kids were already climbing like monkeys.

Sophia brushed off a swing, then sat down and pushed it into motion with her feet. She watched the kids playing while she did. Dahlia wasn't shy at all about asking Darryl to help her up the ladder into the tower on top of the set. Not that she needed any help at all, as she demonstrated by careening down the slide, and then scurrying back up the ladder again all by herself.

No longer needed, Darryl came and sat on the empty swing beside Sophia's. "I owe you an apology."

"Yes, you do," she said. She was in a playful, happy, holiday mood. Thanks to this crazy huge family. "I hope that wasn't it."

He sighed, lowered his head. He was sitting still on the swing, but she was rocking back and forth on hers, not too high. Just high enough. When he lifted his head again he said, "I'm sorry I wasn't honest with you."

"Nope, not gonna cut it. Not only is it insincere, but it wasn't the least bit creative. You can do better."

He seemed surprised. "It's very sincere. I didn't expect there to be…sparks between us, or I'd have told you the truth right off the bat."

She rolled her eyes. "Pointless sparks, since you can hardly wait to get back to Texas." Maybe he'd tell her he'd decided to stay here in Big Falls. Maybe he'd ask her to stay, too. So she dangled the bait, but he didn't take it.

"And since you're heading back to New York soon," he said. "That's still the plan, right?" he asked.

"Um-hm." She had to avert her eyes. She didn't like lying, so she said, "Probably. I mean, I haven't really decided yet."

"So, then, what were you doing this morning at that big old Victorian on the south edge of town with the for sale sign on the front lawn?"

She glanced at him sideways. "How do you know where I was this morning? Still spying on me for my cousins?"

"Not for your cousins, no."

She frowned, preparing to ask what that was supposed to mean, but he went on before she could. "I was passing by and saw your car. Noticed that place had another sign on the lawn. 'Big Falls Family Clinic.'"

Sophia shrugged. "I was just curious. That's all. Sunny, from the bakery, says the local doctor is retiring and moving to Boca."

"So then, you're thinking seriously about staying?"

She hated to be the first one in the water here, but she decided there was no point playing it cagey with him. He was too sharp. "Yeah, I am thinking about it." Then she sent him a pointed look. "What about you, Darryl? Why are you still here?"

"I was hungry and I was invited."

She shook her head. "I didn't mean here at Bobby Joe and Vidalia's local version of the North Pole. I meant here in Big Falls. I thought you'd leave once your job of spying on me was over."

"Watching over you, not spying on you," he corrected. Then he shrugged. "The guys wanted two weeks to find a replacement."

She narrowed her eyes on him and he looked away. "You're not cooking up a scheme to keep right on playing big strong male to the poor helpless little damsel in distress, are you?"

He shook his head solemnly.

"Why don't I believe you?"

"Because you don't trust me. And that's probably my fault for being less than honest at the start."

Sensing an opening, she stopped her swing. "Maybe I'd trust you more if I knew more about you," she said.

"I'm pretty much an open book. What do you want to know?"

Sophia pounced on the opening like a kitten on a catnip mouse. "What made you so sad that you wrote that heartbreakingly beautiful Christmas song of yours?"

Darryl looked toward the house, then back at the kids, climbing on the monkey bars and laughing out loud. A little pang hit him in the gut. He sighed heavily. "That song was inspired by a tough time in my life."

"So you loved someone, and then you lost them?"

"Something like that."

"But it must've been a long time ago, right?"

"Yeah. Seventeen years."

She tilted her head to one side, but then she pushed her swing into motion again. He watched her swinging back and forth past him as he sat still. The way her hair moved, the way she straightened her legs, toes turned inward as she swung forward, then bending her knees as she swung back. She was enjoying herself. But she was also listening to him with every part of her.

"She must've been something, if you're still hung up on her after seventeen years."

He didn't say anything for a long time. Then, looking at the kids, not at her, maybe because it gave him courage, he said, "It wasn't like that. I was a kid. She was a kid. She got pregnant. I wanted to get married. But she wasn't ready."

"So what happened?"

He closed his eyes, kept his face turned away from hers. "She ended it."

"The relationship?"

"The pregnancy."

Sophia put her feet down and brought her swing to a stop. He knew it, but still couldn't look at her. "I'm so sorry, Darryl."

He nodded, "Me, too. I should be over it by now, I'm aware of that. It's just..."

He stopped there. Sophie reached out a hand, touched his cheek like she was brushing something off it. He was compelled to meet her eyes. "Just what?" she asked.

He nodded, having decided to talk about it for the first time, and not even sure why. Unless it was just because of her. "I enlisted right after I found out—shipped out a few months later.

The truck I was riding in got blown up. I took some shrapnel and…long story short, I'll never be a father."

She got off her swing and came around to stand in front of his. He held her gaze because there wasn't much choice and he didn't want to come off as a coward. Maybe his eyes were a little damp, but what the hell. "I've never told anyone that, besides my sister," he said. "I probably wouldn't have told her, but she was with me through most of it. So she knew."

"I'm so sorry, Darryl. That's a horrible thing to have to live with."

He nodded. "It was Christmastime when it all went down. Christmas day when the truck I was in hit that IED. I had expected to be spending that Christmas with my kid, you know?" He sighed. "I wrote that song while I was still flat on my back. After that, I guess I just started avoiding reminders of that time in my life. And that made me tend to avoid all the holiday hoopla."

"Not easy to do in Big Falls. Worse yet over in Tucker Lake."

"Yeah? You think they're more Christmassy than you?"

"Only because there are more of 'em." She smiled, but it didn't meet her eyes, and then they went all sad again. "Must've about ripped out your heart when I made the band play your song the other night. I'm sorry about that."

"You didn't know."

"No, but I wanted to."

He frowned, a little bit distracted from the old ache. Hell, he was so used to it, he barely noticed it anymore. It was just always with him. That empty spot in his heart. "You wanted to?"

She nodded. "I was trying to figure you out. Thought if I played your song, you might…I don't know. Give something away."

"I guess I did."

One of the kids began to howl, though, so he was saved from having to say more. He jumped off his swing and two quick strides brought him to the top of the slide where Cal and his twin sister were both vying to go down first. He quickly gripped the little boy around the waist and scooped him up high in the air, spinning in a circle and making airplane noises. The kid stopped howling and started laughing.

Smiling, Sophie crouched at the bottom of the slide and urged Dahlia to come down. She did, giggling all the way, and then as Sophie caught her and swept her away, Darryl dropped the little boy at the top for his turn.

As he did, he looked down at Sophie, found her eyes on his. She said, "I've learned something since I've been back here in Big Falls, you know."

"Don't tell me. It's all that everything-happens-for-a-reason stuff you were spouting the other day," he said.

She nodded. "I doubted it too, at first. But I'm starting to think it's for real. Maybe nothing's truly impossible. Maybe things have a way of working out the way they're supposed to. Maybe if you're meant to father a child, you will."

"Right, despite a medically necessary vasectomy?"

"Maybe you've just got to believe."

"You really think that?"

She raised her eyebrows. "I didn't used to. But my first day back here...I had a long talk with a wise old man. He said I came back here for a reason. And then I got here, and everything bad that drove me out of New York went away. I started sleeping at night again. I started feeling peaceful again. I found out the local doc is retiring and the town needs a replacement." She lowered her lashes to cover her eyes. "I met you."

He felt a warm rush of feeling sort of pooling up in his chest.

"Santa Claus was right, Darryl. He was right about everything."

"Santa Claus?"

She nodded. "He was the one who told me all of this stuff. So I wrote him a letter, just like I used to when I was a little girl.

And everything I put in there is happening for me. I think maybe I really do belong here. I think maybe…I was led here. I feel like my eyes have been opened. All of a sudden everything looks different. I can trace back every event in my life and see how they had to be just what they were in order to get me where I wanted to go next. And now I'm here, and the life I was meant to live seems close. Closer than ever before."

He sat real still on his swing, staring at her, his brain trying to process everything she'd said.

"I think I belong here in Big Falls, Darryl. I think I'm going to buy that big Victorian and set up a family practice right there where it's always been. And that's the first time I've said that to anyone."

She smiled, and he could read her face perfectly. She'd made that decision just then. She'd made it with him. That felt really good. Then she leaned back and pushed her swing into motion again. Her eyes fell closed, and her hair flew behind her.

"Miracles abound, Darryl," she said real softly. "Especially this time of year. They're everywhere you look. All you have to do is let yourself hope, that's close enough to believing. Just let yourself hope it might be true. And maybe…maybe write your own letter to Santa Claus. It sure has worked for me." She looked at him briefly as she passed and added, "So far."

CHAPTER TWELVE

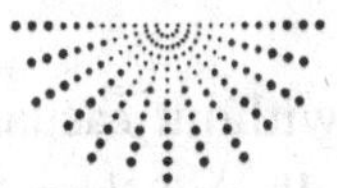

$\mathcal{D}$arryl's pickup truck growled nicely as he drove it around behind the Long Branch and sat there letting it idle. He revved it a little and felt a deep sense of pleasure at the sound. He'd done that—made that engine sound that way, given it all that power. He'd installed the lift kit, added the huge tires. His truck was his pride and joy.

He wished he understood himself as well as he understood his truck. He'd thought he had a pretty good grip on things. But the things his beautiful Sophie had said on the backyard swing had his brain spinning. How could she seriously believe that everything was part of some kind of master plan? He'd lost his chance at fatherhood, forever, for crying out loud.

He shut the engine down, got out of the truck and took his leftovers with him as he headed up the outside staircase that led to the second floor. The McIntyre fellas had decided they didn't want their overnight guests forced to walk through the saloon every time they came or went. Although, so far those "guests" were Joey and Robert themselves, and him. For the moment.

He unlocked the door and wondered if Sophie could, by any

stretch of the imagination, be onto something. She sure as hell seemed happier than she'd been when he'd first met her.

Three containers full of leftovers were balanced between his left arm and his chest, and when the stack wobbled he froze halfway through the door. A bolt of terror shot through him at the thought of any of those treasures hitting the floor. Pumpkin Pie. A thick slice of ham. A vat of gravy-soaked potatoes. Precious cargo.

He adjusted his grip without casualties, sighed in relief and went inside, down the hall, and then into his small room. The guys had set him up a mini-fridge and he took his treasures to it, then fished the small baby food jar full of homemade whipped cream out of his pocket and put that inside as well.

Losing that baby and then the ability to produce any more, had led him to write *Christmas Blues*. The song had gone on to become the biggest success of his entire life and earned him a CMA for song of the year.

His grandfather used to say that no one ever died before their time. He used to say everyone has a purpose and once it's fulfilled, they go back and start over. Even children, he'd said. What if that was true?

Had he been grieving something that had never been a part of the plan? Had his heart been broken by things that happened exactly the way they were supposed to happen, as Sophie's Santa Claus had told her?

He didn't believe it. It didn't make sense to believe life could be that simple. But he couldn't get it out of his head that he had to explore this notion a little bit. He let himself wonder…what if it was true?

What if it was true? What would that mean for him?

He walked into the bathroom in sort of a daze and stared at himself in the mirror. He saw himself as if he was looking at a stranger. Nice, square jaw. Strong jaw. He liked his jaw, he decided.

Then he focused on his eyes, stared hard right into them, and he realized that there was a whole person underneath the mask he'd been wearing since he'd come home from the Middle East. The mask he wore was made of grief, anger and regret because of what had been taken from him.

But what if that was meant to be, as well? And who was the real him, without all of that? Who would he be right now, if those tragedies hadn't happened to him?

He looked across the room. His guitar case stood in the corner near the bed. He took it everywhere he went, but he hadn't played in months. Just hadn't felt...alive enough to play. Not in a long time now. Oh, he'd pick it up, strum a few chords, think about writing another song. But it never went anywhere. He hadn't written anything since "Christmas Blues." He had only just begun to feel the urge again, since coming here to Big Falls.

Since meeting Sophie.

And all of the sudden, right then, it was more than an urge. It was a need.

He walked to the guitar case and crouched, flipped the latches and opened the lid. Then he closed his hand around the neck of his gleaming Gibson and took her out. He cradled the instrument in his arms and let his fingers pluck the strings as he tuned them.

A long, long breath sighed from his lungs. It felt like he'd been holding it for years.

Sophia said she had left some things she needed back at the Long Branch and left right after dessert. Darryl had been oddly quiet throughout the meal and had taken his dessert to go, because Vidalia wouldn't let him leave without it. His early exit *might* have been because of the amount of food he'd packed away. Holy Moses, that man could eat. Then again, Vidalia was a legendary cook, according to Uncle Bobby Joe. Sophia had figured he was just bragging at first, but the woman lived up to every bit of it and then some.

She felt happy as she drove back through town, over the now familiar streets, past the stores and shops. The decision she'd made tonight, to buy that house, to set up a medical practice there, to make Big Falls her forever home, felt right, all the way to her bones. An overwhelming sense of peace had settled into her the second she'd blurted the words to Darryl. It was right. She was where she was supposed to be. Life was good. She was going to be okay.

And there was something else going on too, something big. She was pretty sure she was falling in love with Darryl Champlain. Everything she'd wished for in her letter to Santa had come to her. There was just that one last bit on the list. He had to love her too.

For some reason her foot pressed down harder on the accelerator. She drove right past the park and on to the Long Branch. She needed to see Darryl.She parked right beside his truck in the back, used her keys to let herself into the saloon and hurried through the empty place. Chairs were upturned on top of tables and the whole place was in shadow. There wasn't a sound until she headed up the stairs. And that's when the soft strums of a guitar floated to her, the chords changed, and a rhythm seemed to take form.

And she heard Darryl, his voice, deep and little bit raspy, as he began to sing.

She believes in fairytales
She believes in magic
She believes that dreams come true.
All fantasy, but when I see
Those eyes of sparklin' blue

Damned if I don't start believin' too.

She stood there on the stairs with a dopey smile on her face, her heart beating like a butterfly's wings. Damn. *Damn,* life was good.

She forced herself the rest of the way up the stairs and stood outside his door, waiting to see if he would play some more, and when the silence stretched out, she knocked softly.

She heard his footsteps, heavy and even, and then the door opened, and he looked into her eyes and she looked right back into his. He wrapped his arms around her waist and pulled her inside and right up against him.

Then he was kissing her, and she was kissing him back. She clasped the back of his head in her hands. He kicked the door closed, then slid both hands down her back and down to her thighs. He pulled her legs up around his waist, and carried her to the bed. They fell into it together, and she laughed as she started to unbutton his shirt.

"I heard you playing. It blew me away."

"I just wrote it."

"It's good. It'll win you another award."

"Yeah, well, I'll give credit to my muse."

She smiled. "You mean me?"

"I mean you." He stopped kissing her for long enough to gaze into her eyes. He looked worried, concerned, hesitant. He was about to say something she was sure she didn't want to hear, so she lowered herself on top of him and resumed kissing his face. And they didn't talk again for a long time.

The Long Branch was open on Christmas Eve because the Brands, and apparently the McIntyres too, loved Christmas and wanted to share that with the whole town. Everyone showed up.

The music teacher from the local high school played the piano, and carols were sung around the tree. Festive drinks were on the house, and a buffet dinner was served at cost.

Darryl stood watching the crowd, or trying to. Mostly his eyes were on Sophie behind the bar. Damn, she could sling drinks.

Nothing had changed, though. Not really. He was still carrying the burden of his past, the regret and the anger. She was a happy, hopeful romantic who believed in miracles. He was a realist. Oh, he'd had one weak moment, after she'd left him last night. He'd actually written a Dear Santa letter of his own. It was in the glove box of his truck right now. Stupid. The whole thing, the notion of him and her together—it would never work. He would bring her down. She could do better.

Jason walked up and clapped him on the shoulder. "What do you think of our Christmas Eve bash?" he asked.

"Just wondering how you all make it home in time for the reindeer on the roof," he replied. It was a great event, truly. Everyone in the crowded saloon was happy, laughing.

"Oh, it only goes till nine," Jason said. "Then we close down until the twenty-sixth, and we have shortened hours from then till the second. More time for you to stare at my pretty cousin."

Darryl blinked and realized that was exactly what he'd been doing the entire time Jason had been talking to him. "Sorry. It isn't—"

"The hell it isn't." Jason sighed. "She feel the same way?"

"I think so."

"So what are you waiting for?"

He shook his head. "I'm not the kind of guy she deserves." Darryl couldn't believe he'd just blurted that. It wasn't the kind of thing a guy like him said out loud. It was the kind of thing he only put into a song.

But then Jason said, "It's never too late to change, you know."

Something drew his eyes back to Sophie. She was taking off her apron and hurrying out from behind the bar, then through the crowded dance floor toward the batwing doors.

"Where the hell is she going?" Jason wondered out loud. He started to move, but Darryl put a hand on his shoulder.

"I got this." Jason frowned at him but Darryl said, "I'm still the bouncer—head of security, I mean. It's my job." Then he went after her. She was outside and out of sight by the time he stepped through the still-swinging doors, and for some reason that made him nervous.

He went out through the exterior door and into the front parking lot. It was dark, and snowflakes were dancing their way from the sky to the ground, coating the lot full of cars and the sidewalk and pavement. Snow on Christmas Eve. Wasn't that something?

He heard Sophie's heels clicking on the blacktop, followed the sound, and caught up with her quickly, just as she was unlocking her car. "Everything okay, Sophie?"

She jumped and spun around, one hand on her chest. Then she started laughing and leaned back on her car. "You scared the jingle bells outta me."

"Sorry." He walked closer. "You're starting to sound like your Aunt Vidalia."

Something moved several yards behind Sophie's right shoulder, and he squinted that way.

"There are worse things than sounding like her," she said. "Though looking like her at her age would be my preference."

He didn't say anything, and when the silence stretched, snapped his eyes back to hers. "You don't have anything to worry about in that department, lady." Before he even finished saying it, he was looking past her again.

"Could'a fooled me," she said.

"Go on inside, okay? I need to check something out."

She turned around as soon as he said it, looking where he was looking, toward a barely visible shape, a human shape, in the shadows behind the cars. And then suddenly, the shadow burst into motion.

"Get inside!" he said, and he lunged after it. He lengthened his strides and pushed harder, and within a few seconds, he was tackling the hoodie-wearing stalker to the ground.

"Darryl, dammit, don't you hurt him!" Sophie shouted from way closer than she ought to be. "Be careful, for crying out—"

Momentarily glancing Sophie's way was a fatal mistake. The kid socked him in the jaw, knocking Darryl off him and springing upright. Then he took off running.

Darryl got up, rubbing his jaw and staring off down the street where the kid had gone. "Dammit, Sophie, this guy is up to something. Are you not getting it? How many times have I seen him lurking around you now? Who skulks in the shadows on Christmas Eve, Sophie? Who? Huh?"

She didn't answer and the kid was long gone, so he turned around.

Sophia was holding a sheet of creased paper close to her face, squinting to read it in the dim parking lot lights. Then she clapped a hand over her mouth and her wide eyes shot to his.

"What?" he asked.

"He...dropped this." She held the paper out to him. "You'd better read it, Darryl."

So Darryl took the letter from her hand and turned his back to the nearest overhead light so it fell on the pretty penmanship scrawled across the lined sheet.

My Darling Max,

I wish I had the courage to tell you this to your face, but I just don't. I'm so afraid you'll hate me for it. And now that I know I'm not going to be here much longer, I don't want to waste what time we have left together fixing this. Selfish of me, I know.

So now that I'm gone, you need to know the truth. Your father isn't dead, as I always told you he was. Your father is alive. His name is Darryl Champlain, and he's a little bit famous for writing a country song. Last I knew he was a cop in Houston. I never told him about you. He knew I was pregnant, but I told him I'd ended it. He wanted to get married, settle down, raise you together, and I just wasn't ready for that. I planned to give you up for adoption, and I was afraid he'd fight me on it. So I lied to him.

And then you were born, and I held you in my arms and I knew I couldn't let you go.

I've kept this secret from you for seventeen years, and for that I'm sorry. I love you. I have always loved you and I always will. And I'm watching over you, my darling son. Never doubt it.

Love,

Mom

Darryl lifted his head, blinking in shock.

"You um," Sophie sniffed and wiped a tear from her cheek. "You didn't happen to try that…that hoping thing I suggested, did you Darryl?"

He met her eyes and felt his heart sort of swell. "Yeah," he said. "I did." He smiled. And then his smile died, and he looked off into the distance the kid—his *son*—Max—had gone.

"I've gotta find him!"

"We'll find him, don't worry. Go on, go after him. I'll get the family."

"They don't have to—it's Christmas Eve, I can't ask them to—"

"Yeah, it's kind of a thing with this family. They—I mean, we —stick together. Even the black sheep eventually come back to the flock. I can't break with tradition. Go on, go after your son.

We'll be right behind you." Then she stood up on tiptoes, and said, "*I'll* be right behind you, Darryl. For as long you want me there." She kissed him. Then she turned and ran back inside the Long Branch.

Darryl folded and pocketed the boy's letter while heading around the saloon for his truck in the back. By God, he had a son. He had a son!

CHAPTER THIRTEEN

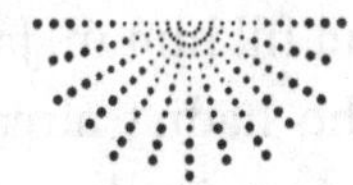

Sophie headed back inside, and went around behind the bar, ignoring the drink orders shouted her way from those who surrounded it. Grabbing the remote from its holster on the way past, she braced her hands on the mahogany, and sprung up onto the bar top. Then she thumbed the remote, silencing the music. She put her fingers to her lips and cut a shrill whistle. "I need the Brand-McIntyre clan in the kitchen."

Then she jumped down and headed in there herself.

Within minutes they were all crammed into the kitchen, and Ned, the saggy faced old cook was sent scurrying out to do what he could for the customers. Vidalia and Bobby Joe, Vidalia's five daughters and five sons in law, Caleb's father Cain, Selene's brother-in-law Casey, Jimmy's best friend Colby, Sophie's cousins Jason, Rob, and Joey surrounded her.

Her family.

She got a lump in her throat, and knew this was right where she belonged. She cleared her throat and said, "There's a teenage boy out there and he might be in trouble. His name is Max and his mom died recently. He's all alone and it's Christmas Eve. Will you guys help me look for him?

"Dang straight we will," Vidalia shouted.

There was immediate, noisy agreement, and Sophie told everyone what the boy looked like and where she'd last seen him. She saw curious looks when she mentioned that Darryl had already gone after the kid, but no one asked questions. They just nodded and headed out. Kara's husband Jimmy Corona worked for Big Falls' tiny police department, and said he'd contact Chief Wheatly and fill him in. Jason and Joey said they'd see to the few guests who hadn't already left the saloon, and then would head out to join in the search. Everyone jumped into action.

And all she'd had to do was ask.

Yeah, this was where she belonged. Here, with this amazing bunch. No question about it. And she was pretty sure Darryl and Max belonged here too. She hoped they would agree.

It had been hours. Darryl had been in almost constant contact with Sophie, who relayed to him which roads were being searched by which of her family members. Every back road and rural route, logging trail and cow path within a ten-mile radius of Big Falls was being covered. He felt as if he'd driven over most of them himself. And yet, there was no sign of Max. No sign at all.

Darryl was dejected. He was desperate. What if Max had gone off road, out into the middle of nowhere? There was lot of nowhere around Big Falls. A kid could get lost forever out there. And it was cold tonight, and still snowing a little bit.

His phone pinged, and he glanced down at the message screen.

Sophie: *Don't forget to believe.*

He sighed. Right. Okay, well, why the hell not?

"I believe I'm gonna find him. I believe I'm gonna find him. I'm gonna find him."

What he couldn't believe was that he was saying that to himself over and over as he drove through the center of Big Falls. Every single building was decked in holiday lights. Every lamp post bore a twinkling wreath, gleaming cheerfully in the darkness of the night. All the way up ahead in that round little park in the town's center, the towering evergreen just twinkled and glowed.

He needed to turn around. He needed to head back out of town, and recheck some of the back roads. But it was easier to keep going and loop around the park than to execute a three-point turn in his truck. So he did. And that's when he saw the kid, right there on the bench, huddled against the cold and staring up at the giant Christmas tree.

The boy didn't look his way when Darryl cut the engine and headlights. He took Max's letter from his pocket, and then, almost as an afterthought, he opened the glove box and took out the other letter. The one he'd sealed in an envelope last night, after Sophie had left him, but never intended to mail anywhere.

He got out and closed the door, then walked slowly over to the boy, trying to see his face in the gentle glow of the Christmas tree lights. When he got to the bench, the kid sat up straighter, still not looking at him. Darryl sat down beside him, took a deep breath. "You dropped your mom's letter," he said, holding it out.

The kid nodded, took it, crammed it into his own pocket.

"I didn't know. I never knew," Darryl said. "I'm really sorry about back there. Sophie, she's got an ex with bad habits, and I thought he might've sent someone after her. I'm really sorry."

The kid just nodded. His face was empty, but bore the marks of tears. It was a knife in Darryl's heart to think of him sitting here in the cold, all alone, orphaned by his mom, attacked by his father, staring almost accusingly at a lighted tree on Christmas Eve.

"You must be feeling like all this Christmas magic is just one big pile of bull, about now, huh? I've been feeling that way too. For a long time."

Max shrugged, still not looking at him.

"I've been trying to figure out what to say to you ever since I read that letter," Darryl said. "But I think maybe you should read this. I think maybe this will tell you everything a lot more easily than I will if I keep running my mouth." He pulled the envelope from his pocket, held it out. "I wrote it last night. A friend of mine—well more than a friend—she told me it worked for her." He shook the envelope. "Go on, read it."

The boy looked at him. First time. He looked right into his eyes. He was damn good looking, if Darryl could trust his own judgment. An oval face, strong jaw, kind eyes that might be deep blue like his own, but right then, only reflected the twinkling colors of the tree. So very wounded, those eyes.

Max, Darryl thought. My son.

"Please?" he asked. "Please read it?"

Nodding, Max took the envelope and tore it open. He unfolded the note, and glanced down. Darryl knew exactly what it said.

Dear Santa,

I only want two things for Christmas, and they're both impossible. I don't even know why I'm writing this, except that Sophie has a way of making me want to believe. So here goes. I want to be a father, and I want to be a good enough man to deserve to marry Sophie McIntyre.

That was all the note said, besides his scribbled signature.

The kid looked up and right into his eyes. "You...wrote this yesterday?"

"Yeah. I um, I got injured in Iraq. I can't have kids. And I thought you...I thought I'd lost you, before you were even born."

There was silence for a long moment, then Max said, "Do you remember my mom?"

"Oh, do I ever." He looked at the kid, knew he was craving more than just that, so he went on. "She was the most beautiful girl in the state of Texas. Prom queen. I was nuts about her. So was every other guy in our high school." He lowered his head. "I'm real sorry you lost her, Max. She was something special."

Max lowered his head.

Darryl reached out a hand, put in on his shoulder. "You're not alone anymore. I'm your father. I'm here for you."

Max knuckled his eyes, nodded without looking up. "I didn't...I didn't think you'd want me. You don't have to—"

"Want you? I wished for you. You're on my letter to the Claus, how much clearer could it be? Max...I can hardly believe this is happening. You're my...okay, this is sappy as hell, but it's the truth. You're my miracle."

The boy finally lifted his head. His eyes were wet, but he smiled through his tears. Darryl hugged him, clapping his back, holding on tight. "We'll stick together from now on, okay? You and me."

Max pulled back, wiped his cheeks, looked down at the letter in his hand. "And maybe Sophie, huh?"

"I don't know, man. You think Santa's good for more than one wish come true a year?"

"I didn't used to think he was good for even one," Max said.

Darryl's already wet eyes got wetter and a tear spilled over. He was pretty sure Max must mean he'd wished for him too. He pulled out his phone. "I've gotta let her know I found you. She's got her entire family out looking."

"Really?"

"Oh, yeah. And if I get my second wish, that pile of rednecks is gonna be your family too. Just a heads-up."

Then he texted her. *I found him.*

"I see that," Sophie said from nearby. He glanced up to see her walking toward them. Her car was parked behind his truck on the road, and he hadn't even heard her pull up.

Max elbowed him. "I'll go so you can ask her."

"Ask her…no, no, not yet. Not yet. I want to show her the new me first. The happy guy, the guy who believes in magic." He smiled at his son. "I do, you know. She kept telling me and I didn't believe her, but now…."

He clapped the boy on the shoulder, and said, "Come on."

They both got up and met Sophie as she hurried toward them, her eyes beaming, her smile irresistible.

"Sophie, I'd like you to meet Max. My son." Then he looked sideways at his kid. "Max, this is Sophia McIntyre, the woman I love."

Sophie's smile died and her eyes rounded. She jerked her eyes from Max to lock onto Darryl's.

Max said, "Nice to meet you Sophia."

"You can call me Sophie," she said, finally managing to tear her eyes off Darryl to look at his son again. "You know you're a walking miracle, don't you? You are your dad's Christmas wish come true."

"Only half of it," he said. Then he bumped his shoulder into Darryl's and said, "You should show her the letter."

"What letter?"

Max handed an envelope to Darryl and said, "I'm cold. Can I, uh—"

"You can wait in the truck if you want, Max," Darryl said. "I won't be long."

The boy nodded and headed away from them. Darryl heard

the pickup door close. He was still standing there, staring into Sophie's eyes. He could see the Christmas tree lights twinkling their reflection there.

She said, "You wrote a letter to Santa, didn't you?"

"I did."

"And it worked, didn't it?"

"Remains to be seen."

"You mean you didn't ask for Max?"

"Yeah, I did. And I got him. And I have you to thank for that."

She shook her head. "You have *you* to thank for that." Then she frowned. "And Santa, too!"

"Maybe."

"Don't tell me you still have doubts. You got what you asked for."

"Not *everything* I asked for." He slid his arms around her waist. "I kind of made a big declaration there a minute ago."

She smiled hugely, sliding her hands over his shoulders. "You sure did."

"You got anything to say back?" he whispered, moving his mouth closer to hers.

"I sure do," she said, her lips brushing his with the words.

"Well, say it, then."

She smiled against his mouth. "Merry Christmas," she whispered.

Laughing, he kissed her, bending her backwards and holding her close. When he paused for a breath, she said, "And I love you too."

He picked her up and spun her around in a circle. When he set her down again, she grabbed his hand and tugged him with her to the waiting truck. She opened the passenger door and smiled in at Max. "You guys can follow me back to Vidalia and Bobby Joe's. They have plenty of room, and this way we'll all be together for Christmas."

Then she looked from Max to Darryl and back again. "It'll be our first Christmas together. And if *my* Christmas wishes all come true, it'll be the first of many."

The boy looked relieved, nervous, and tired.

Darryl said, "I didn't have time to shop for you, son. But I've got seventeen years' worth of Christmas presents to make up for, so I'm gonna give you one very big one this year." Then he handed his pickup keys to Max. "Hope you like it."

"What?" The boy blinked. "No way!"

"She's all yours. Um, but you might have to play chauffeur for me until I find alternative transportation. Shove over, you can drive."

Max gaped, but he shoved over, stuck the keys in the switch, turned it. The motor started up and rumbled.

"Hear that motor? I did that. Supercharged it."

"That's *so* cool."

"I'll teach you how."

Darryl climbed into the passenger seat and Sophie climbed up after him, gripped his collar, and kissed his face. He pulled her across his lap and said, "Ride with us. We can get your car in the morning."

"Okay."

He reached out to pull the door closed, then paused, frowning. "Wait, wait. Do you hear that?"

Max frowned, but turned off the ignition to listen. Sophie cocked her head to one side. "Are those…are those sleigh bells?"

"Look!" Max shouted, pointing skyward.

There was something…a flash, a streak of light, a twinkle, and then just the starry sky, as empty as if nothing had ever been there.

Darryl looked at Sophie. She closed her eyes and whispered, "Thank you, Santa Claus. Merry Christmas."

–THE END–

Continue reading for an excerpt from the next book in
The McIntyre Men Series:

Oklahoma Moonshine

PREVIEW OKLAHOMA MOONSHINE

CHAPTER ONE

Robert McIntyre found the strawberry blonde of his dreams out behind the Long Branch Saloon, near the trash cans. She was bending at the waist and twisting sideways, using her cell phone's glow to try to see the back of her left thigh and holding her skirt up high in the effort. As a result, he could see the full length of her long leg from the shapely calf emerging from the top of her cowgirl boot to the sexy curve of her thigh.

He stopped looking by sheer force of will, cleared his throat and said,

"Can I uh, help you with something?"

She straightened, gasped, dropped the skirt and damn near jumped out of it all at once. He held up both hands, "Easy, I'm just one of the owners, taking out the trash." He held up his plastic bag as if to prove it, and reminded himself that she wasn't the woman of his dreams. He didn't dream about women. He had nightmares about them.

She blinked at him for a second, then smiled, patting her chest with her hand. "You scared me half outta my boots."

He was getting sucked into that big white smile, so he lowered his head as if to inspect said boots as he carried the overstuffed bag to the trash can nearest her, took off the lid and dropped it inside.

Cowgirl boots, they were. Brown leather with pink embroidery and heels that would challenge a tightrope walker.

"I was s'posed to meet an old friend here for a nightcap," she said. "But I guess she's not coming. I walked around back looking for a few more bars on my phone, and caught my skirt on a branch. I think a thorn got my leg."

For some reason, every bit of it seemed false, and alarm bells sounded in his head. "You uh—need me to check for you?"

Her brows rose high over those big, innocent eyes. In the overhead lamplight, he thought he saw freckles across the bridge of her nose.

"Are you flirting with me?"

He blinked. "I don't think so. But if you're here for that nightcap, we're closed."

"Oh." She lowered her head. Wavy ribbons of pale honey and sunshine fell down over her cheek.

"I'm the only one here. Otherwise I'd invite you in."

"I don't mind that you're the only one here," she said, real fast and eager. And she beamed those eyes at him, all full of hope. "I mean, you're one of the McIntyres, aren't you?"

"Rob," he said nodding.

"Kiley," she said, extending a hand.

He took it. She had a nice hand, soft and warm, and she gripped his all snug and strong. She had an honest handshake. That was a good sign, right?

"Everyone knows you McIntyres are upright citizens. I'm not scared to be alone with you. And I sure could use that nightcap."

He had no freaking idea why he was grinning like a friendly

chimp, and he quickly tried to press his mouth into a straight line. "Come on in. I could use one, too." Stupid, stupid, stupid, his brain said. He extended an elbow and she grabbed onto it, walking close enough that her perfume made his brain go fuzzy. Maybe not so stupid, he thought.

They crossed the brand new deck, and he opened the door for her, then watched her as she sashayed on through, her skirt swaying, her boots tapping the floor. The big lights were all turned off, but there were night lights on. They were spaced evenly at floor level throughout every room at the Long Branch. As they walked through the kitchen, the counters and dangling pots and pans, and giant cook surfaces and sinks and coolers were all easy to distinguish. "This way," he said, guiding her toward the big double doors, then through them into the barroom.

It was dimmer there, and all the chairs had been tipped up on top of the tables. He walked her right up to the bar, and she slid onto a saddle shaped stool, sidesaddle style.

Rob went behind the bar. "What can I get you?"

"Rum and Coke. Helps me sleep."

He made her a drink, grabbed himself a long neck, and stayed on his own side of the bar. "You don't sleep well, huh?"

"Not tonight. Tonight my dream is circling the drain." She held up her glass. "Here's to believing in last minute miracles."

He tapped her glass with the top of his brown bottle and took a nice long pull from it.

She looked around the bar, pointed at the giant cardboard sign near the jukebox and said, "I've been seeing signs like that all over town. What's it about?"

The cardboard thermometer measured dollars instead of degrees. It was painted red all the way from $0 to $275,000, but the word "goal" was way up at the $500,000 mark. She read the lines across the top aloud. "'Big Falls' Big Future?'"

"People are worried about drought," he explained. "It's been bad south of here, and forecasters say it's coming our way, sooner or later. So the town's raising funds to buy some property and build a reservoir. The land's for sale at three-hundred and fifty, and the rest is to get the building underway."

"I wouldn't have thought a small town like this would be able to raise so much."

"I'm surprised too. The church is giving half its bingo proceeds, firemen are holding chili socials. Every business in town is chipping in what they can. When anyone buys property here, the Post Office automatically sends them a flyer asking for a contribution. Even little kids are selling lemonade for the cause."

"That's nice, everyone pulling together like that." Except she was frowning at that sign like she wished she could see through it.

"It's that kind of town."

"Yeah. Yeah, it is, isn't it?" She studied her drink, turning the glass slowly on its coaster. "I grew up here. Well, 'til I was thirteen anyway. Long time ago. I didn't realize how much I missed it until I got back here."

He nodded slow. "Big Falls has a way of getting inside a person. I never intended to stay here either. But now...." He shrugged, deciding not to go on, or he'd start sounding like he believed the local tales about a town that chose its residents and refused to let them go. "You gonna tell me about this dream of yours that's in danger of imminent demise?"

She smiled at him. He thought there should have been a ricochet sound effect to go with that smile when she aimed it his way.

"What is it about sitting at a bar that makes people want to whine about their troubles to the guy on the other side?"

"I don't know, hon, but there's no point bucking tradition, is there?" He found a clean bowl, scooped it full of bar mix from the canister, and set it in front of her. "Whine away."

She smiled at him. "You're a nice guy, aren't you?"

"No. I'm brooding and grouchy. Ask my brothers."

"I will." She pinched a pretzel out of the bowl, ate it, sighed. "You know the old Kellogg place, out on Pine Road?"

"Hell yeah, I know it." In fact, he'd been out there earlier in the week, looking at the ranch with Betty Lou Jennings, Big Falls' resident gossip queen and only real estate agent. The Kellogg property was a thousand acres of prime ground; lush meadows with the Cimarron River running right through it, three ponds, and a hundred-acre woodlot, two barns and a sweet little farmhouse, all about to be auctioned off for back taxes.

"Beautiful, isn't it?" she asked. And she tipped her head sideways and gazed off into space, like she was seeing it in her mind's eye. "That old-fashioned farmhouse with the flower boxes in front, and those shutters with the heart shaped cutouts in them, and the way the porch wraps around one side...."

In his mind, those heart shaped cutouts in the shutters were gonna be the first things to go. He didn't bother telling her so, but he had a feeling a strawberry blond storm cloud was about to start raining on his plans. And when she spoke again, it did.

"I was planning to buy it. They're auctioning it off tomorrow, you know."

"Yeah. I know." He was planning to bid on it himself, on his own, not with the trust fund his father had set up for each of his sons, funds so big they were snowballing under the momentum of their own interest and dividends now.

He wanted to buy the ranch with his own money. Not his father's and not some bank's. He'd saved up enough, and he was about 99% sure the old Kellogg place was gonna be the one.

It wasn't in his nature to bid against a beautiful dreamer. But business was business.

"I don't have enough, though," she went on. "Half, maybe." She turned her dewy glass on its coaster, back and forth, back and forth. "Grandma's sending me her heirloom ring, she says it's worth a fortune. There's a jeweler in Tucker Lake who says if the stones are genuine, he'll buy it. But if it doesn't get here by tomorrow morning, before auction time, I'm doomed." She held up her glass, and said, "Here's to the US Postal Service. May it deliver."

"Here, here," he said. But something had changed in her voice and demeanor when she'd started talking about her grandma's ring. Something that told him she was lying, and he couldn't quite figure out why. It was in the way her eyes shifted away when his tried to lock on, and the softer tone.

She took a long sip from her glass, seemed to really relish it, smacked her lips and closed her eyes, and then set the glass down again. "You probably think it's stupid for a woman alone to think she could manage a thousand acres."

"I don't think it's stupid at all. It's a beautiful spread." He gave in to his worse judgment and came out from behind the bar, slid up onto a stool beside her. He could smell her perfume and feel the warmth of her body sort of reaching out to tease his. But he reminded himself that his track record with dishonest women wasn't exactly stellar. "I'm curious though, what would you do with it? Run beefers?"

"I don't want to raise cattle. I've got other things in mind."

He lifted his brows. "What other things?"

"Lambs and bunnies in the spring—for pets, not for eating. An acre-wide patch of shamrock and clover with miniature leprechauns peeking out here and there for St. Patrick's Day, and four-leaf clovers and pots of gold-foiled chocolate hidden for kids to find. I'll host the biggest Easter egg hunt in seven counties at Easter time. I want to try to grow Christmas trees, acres of 'em, so kids can come and pick their own right out of the field. We'll take 'em around on a wagon, or a sleigh those rare seasons when we get a little snow. Maybe have Santa driving it."

"Wow." The way her eyes sparkled while she talked about her plans, the pinkness in her cheeks, those things were damn near taking his breath away.

"I want to landscape the prettiest spot on the place, down by the riverbank, and make it even prettier, then rent it out for folks to hold wedding ceremonies."

"You've really thought this through."

"I've been thinking about it since I was a kid." She lowered her eyes. "I grew up on that ranch. Happier times." She looked up at him and smiled, but it was a sad smile that didn't reach her eyes. "I want to spread my sister's ashes there. But not unless I get the place. If I don't, then… I just want to keep her near me."

And the rainstorm became torrential. How the hell was he going to bid against her now?

"I'm sorry," he said. "Was it recent?"

"Six weeks ago. Almost seven. I don't…I can't—" She held up a hand and her eyes got damp.

Everything in him turned to mush at the sight of those unshed tears. He wanted to chase them away. The power of his attraction to her was shockingly strong. He hadn't felt this drawn to a woman in a long time. Maybe not ever. "Tell me more about your plans for the place."

She sipped her drink, blinked her eyes dry again. "Probably just pipe dreams."

"They don't sound like pipe dreams so far. What about Halloween, what kinds of tricks and treats do you have in mind for Oklahoma Octobers?"

Her whole being shifted, he thought. The light came back into her eyes. "Hayrides and corn mazes and pumpkin patches. The smaller of the two barns would make the most amazing haunted house you ever saw."

"It would, wouldn't it?"

"Mm-hm. I'll name the place Holiday Ranch. It's gonna be a gold mine." She was smiling hugely when she looked his way, then lowered her eyes, her cheeks going pink. "You must think it's a crazy idea."

"I think you might be kind of brilliant."

"Really?" She looked at him as if his answer mattered. "I really want to know. You have a lot more knowledge about business stuff than I do, being the son of RJR McIntyre."

He knew enough about business to be aware that his own dreams for his someday ranch were not likely to be lucrative at all. But he didn't want to do it for the money. "I agree it could be a money maker, after a while. You might be living hand-to-mouth for the first year or two. Might need to grow some sort of crop or lease some of the acreage to a local farmer to help get up on your feet. Might even need to take on a side job until things start rolling. But it's a sound idea. And you're only just scratching the surface of what you can do out there. Gift shop, maybe an on-site coffee and snack bar—"

"Oh, that's good. That's really good." She smiled at him. "Thanks for that. This is important. It's a new beginning for me. A whole new life."

She finished her drink and reached for her handbag.

"Nope. It's on the house."

She smiled up at him, then slid off her stool, landed on the floor, and stumbled a little on those heels. He caught her shoulders and she tipped her head up, met his eyes, and hers turned soft and smoky.

He felt a rush of something warm and dangerous whispering through him. The urge to kiss her was like a giant hand on the back of his head, pushing him closer.

But Rob resisted. "Night, Kiley. It was real nice meeting you."

～

Kiley left that fancy saloon like she was walking on a cloud. She was going to do it. The ranch was practically hers!

Rob McIntyre was polite and sweet and charming, and according to that bumblebee-like real estate agent Betty Lou Jennings, who loved to gossip while showing potential buyers like Kiley around properties, he was very interested in buying the old Kellogg place. He'd be at that auction tomorrow for sure. All she had do was get there ahead of him and wait.

He was more handsome than she'd expected. Yes, she'd seen him from a distance, because she'd been researching him. But up close, it was like being pulled by the force of his gravity or something. He had the sweetest face she thought she'd ever seen. Thick, full lips and a wide broad smile that made his eyes crinkle up. Dark hair that wanted to curl, and just enough scruff on his face to send her hormones into overdrive.

He was so over-the-top nice to her that she'd have suspected he was running a con of his own if she didn't know he was rich. Rich folks could afford to be polite and charming for no reason, she guessed. But it would have been easier if he'd been a jerk to her. Or if he looked like an ogre. Or if his smile hadn't just about made her forget how to breathe.

This was gonna be hard. It would work, but she almost wished it didn't have to.

Kiley Kellogg was turning over a new leaf, going straight, creating a respectable life in her small hometown the way she'd always secretly dreamed of doing. Being that her father was in prison and her sister was dead, she didn't think the message could've been any clearer; she needed to change her life if she didn't want to end up like they had.

But going straight required capital, and she only knew one way to make bank. She'd never been worth a damn at it, nowhere near as good as her dad and Kendra. A constant source of disappointment to them both, as a matter of fact. But if she wanted her home back, she was going to have to up her game.

She had to con a billionaire cowboy into handing her half a million dollars. And she had to do it in a way he would never suspect had been a con at all, because she wanted to go on living in this town once the ranch was hers again. She might even consider paying him back.

She got into her beaten and barely road-worthy car, and then drove it home. It was all of five minutes if you took your time. Right out of the parking lot of The Long Branch Saloon, two miles down, then right onto Pine Road. The ranch her mother had inherited and her father had pissed away, included both sides of Pine road, a full thousand acres of it, wide flat meadows and scrubby woodlots, generously watered by the Cimarron.

Home.

Her battered car's headlights lit the rutted driveway and picked out what remained of stonework pillars on either side. There used to be a gate attached, but it was long gone. Just the rusted hinges remained, their orange-brown decay staining the stones.

She shut the headlights off before driving on through. It wasn't exactly legal to be squatting on the property before she'd bought it, but she couldn't afford much else. The trip from New York had cleaned out most of her cash. Besides what she'd set aside for the auction.

She had five hundred thousand dollars in cash, stuffed into a duffle bag, crammed behind the wall in the back of a bedroom closet. She and Kendra used to hide their diaries in there.

She pulled all the way up to the house, and then drove around behind it, cut the engine and got out. Then she just stood there for a minute, looking around. The sky was so much wider here than in New York, a blanket of twinkling stars, spread as far as you could even see. No moon tonight, and hardly a cloud, either.

When she was a little girl, she and Kendra used to sneak out on nights like this. They'd wander down to where the river meandered through the meadow, and spin until they were too dizzy to stay upright. Then they'd open their arms and fall backward into the deep grass and wildflowers, giggling until it was hard to breathe. When the laughter ebbed, they'd keep lying there. That was the best part. Lying there in the silence of an Oklahoma night, listening to the bullfrogs and grasshoppers and nightbirds, and gazing up at all those stars. Sometimes a fish would jump and splash in the river, or a bullfrog would croon a baritone lullaby.

It would be good to reclaim her home, to be able to live there legally. Good to turn it into what she and Kendra had talked about as kids.

She felt close to her sister there. Closer than she'd felt to her in years. They'd struggled so hard to stay in touch when their father had gone to prison and they'd gone into the system, moving from one foster home to another, never in the same one together. They'd made sure they never fell out of contact back then.

And then they'd turned eighteen and had been booted out on their own. Kendra wanted to run games, con the wealthy, and get rich quick. Kiley wanted to take classes and learn how to make an honest living, so she only grifted when she had no other choice. They'd run one or two fairly successful games together, but they just didn't see things eye to eye. Kiley felt guilty, which made Kendra feel judged. Angry fights ensued, and they'd drifted apart.

She slid her hand into her big handbag and closed it around the black leather drawstring pouch that held Kendra's ashes. "I've just gotta run this one last game to get the rest of the money for the ranch, Sis. Once it's mine and no one can take it, I'll spread your ashes here. Down by the big boulder on the riverbank."

Guilt gnawed at her belly. It was always the same. If she ran a game and failed, which happened more often than not, she hated herself for not living up to her dad's expectations and her sister's phenomenal skills. If she ran a game and succeeded, she felt even worse.

All those people who'd sent her money through *Go-Fund-Yourself.com* for her non-existent Chihuahua's make-believe prosthetic legs, haunted her dreams at night. It had been the most successful con she'd ever played. And it was still only half enough to buy her home back. To fund her dream.

And that was why she had to go straight. She had never been any good at the game anyway. And if she started to *get* good at it, she thought that would be even worse. She just wasn't cut out to be a criminal.

One more game, and she'd have enough to get her home back. And that was it. No more.

Kiley nodded, affirming to herself that all of her dreams were about to come true, and then she went inside, crawling through the same window she'd been using for the past few nights. The house was empty, but had been spruced up for potential buyers. She trailed her fingertips over the fresh paint as she went upstairs to the bedroom that had been her sister's, walked into the closet and pulled away the board that covered up the hollow spot in the wall. Just inside the dark opening her sleeping bag waited, all neatly rolled up. The smaller green duffle contained most of her worldly possessions. Clothes and toiletries, mainly. The bigger green duffle held the cash. She hauled everything out except the cash, and dropped it all onto the bedroom floor.

Her styrofoam ice chest full of food and bottled water stood in the farthest corner from the bedroom windows. There was no electricity turned on in the place, and it was summer and hotter than hell by day. But the century-old farmhouse stayed remarkably cool. Would stay cooler still once she put some curtains in the windows.

She unrolled her sleeping bag, gave it a shake, in case of visitors, then stripped off her clothes, and crawled inside, tired and lonesome, but closer than ever before to her dreams coming true. She just wanted to snuggle down, close her eyes, and imagine how it was going to be.

So she did.

Oklahoma Moonshine

ALSO AVAILABLE

The McIntyre Men
Oklahoma Christmas Blues
Oklahoma Moonshine
Oklahoma Starshine
Shine On Oklahoma
Baby By Christmas
Oklahoma Sunshine

The Oklahoma Brands
The Brands who Came for Christmas
Brand-New Heartache
Secrets and Lies
A Mommy For Christmas
One Magic Summer
Sweet Vidalia Brand

ABOUT THE AUTHOR

New York Times and *USA Today* bestselling novelist Maggie Shayne has published sixty-two novels and twenty-two novellas for five major publishers over the course of twenty-two years. She also spent a year writing for American daytime TV dramas *The Guiding Light* and *As the World Turns*, and was offered the position of co-head writer of the former; a million-dollar offer she tearfully turned down. It was scary, turning down an offer that big. But her heart was in her books, and she'd found it impossible to do both.

In March 2014, she did something even scarier. She left the world's largest publisher and went "indie."

Now, she is embarking on an exciting new leg of her publishing journey, with most of her titles moving to small press publisher, Oliver Heber Books.

Maggie writes small town contemporary romances like the recent *Bliss in Big Falls* series, which boasts "a miracle in every story."

She cut her teeth on western themed category romances like her classic 90s and early 2000s *The Texas Brand* and *The Oklahoma All-Girl Brands,* and later expanded into romantic suspense and thrillers like *The Secrets of Shadow Falls* and *The Brown and de Luca Novels.*

She is perhaps best known for her beloved paranormal romances, like the brand new *Fatal series* and perennial favorites *The Immortals,* the *By Magic series,* and *Wings in the Night.*

Maggie is a fifteen-time RITA® Award nominee and one-time winner. She lives in the rolling green and forested hilltops of Cortland County NY, wine & dairy country, despite having sworn off both. She is a vegan Wiccan hippy living her best life with her beloved husband Lance, and usually at least two dogs.

Maggie also writes spiritual self-help and runs an online magic shop, BlissBlog.org

Visit Maggie at www.maggieshayne.com

www.ingramcontent.com/pod-product-compliance
Lightning Source LLC
Chambersburg PA
CBHW011520100726
47899CB00010BD/3442